The Pursuit of
Miss Heartbreak Hotel

The Pursuit of Miss Heartbreak Hotel

Moe Bonneau

Henry Holt and Company • New York

Henry Holt and Company, *Publishers since 1866*
Henry Holt® is a registered trademark of Macmillan Publishing Group, LLC
175 Fifth Avenue, New York, New York 10010 • fiercereads.com

Library of Congress Cataloging-in-Publication Data
Names: Bonneau, Monique (Designer), author.
Title: The pursuit of Miss Heartbreak Hotel / Moe Bonneau.
Description: First edition. | New York : Henry Holt and Company, 2019. |
    Summary: When Lucy reconnects with her childhood best friend, Eve, in their
    senior year of high school, she is not prepared for the intense emotions—and
    attraction—that follow.
Identifiers: LCCN 2018038777 | ISBN 9781250170934 (hardcover)
Subjects: | CYAC: Best friends—Fiction. | Friendship—Fiction. | Infatuation—Fiction. |
    High schools—Fiction. | Schools—Fiction. | Lesbians—Fiction.
Classification: LCC PZ7.1.B66925 Pur 2019 | DDC [Fic]—dc23
LC record available at https://lccn.loc.gov/2018038777

Our books may be purchased in bulk for promotional, educational, or business
use. Please contact your local bookseller or the Macmillan Corporate and
Premium Sales Department at (800) 221-7945 ext. 5442 or by email at
MacmillanSpecialMarkets@macmillan.com.

First edition, 2019 / Designed by Liz Dresner
Printed in the United States of America
10 9 8 7 6 5 4 3 2 1

And I was green, greener than the hill
Where the flowers grew and the sun shone still
Now I'm darker than the deepest sea
Just hand me down, give me a place to be.

—*Nick Drake*,
"Place to Be"

The Pursuit of
Miss Heartbreak Hotel

Never-Ending Pending Love

In love, there are two ways we break our hearts on someone. Two that I know of, anyway. The first I call Never-Ending Pending Love.

The sharp, lonesome cry of Never-Ending Pending has held me in its grip for as long as I can remember, and in matters of solitude, secrets, and shame I'm a shark, a ringer, a real pro. For the past four years, it's all been for one. For her.

Ms. Hayes.

She's sitting at her desk after school, grading today's five-paragraph essays on *Siddhartha*, furrowing her brow in her hazy, faraway way. She's wearing these tight black leggings and a gigantic, frumpy sweater that could fit at least three other Ms. Hayeses inside and I'm so hit for that great big sweater, I'm always giving her a hard time about it and trying to find ways to steal it and stick my nose in it, memorize the molecules of her siren-song scent.

She peers up at the clock, sighing, and she's delicate and dazzling and golden. She's deep-down sad in the most beautiful way I can ever imagine. She kills me. She really does. She teaches me metaphors, similes, drama, the classics. She's taught me poetry in more ways than one. She's white whale, slick-wet slippery and larger than life, and I'm Ahab and will never have her, but will seek her until I go Ophelia and die.

Up to her elbows in work, I ask her if she's planning on spending the night. She says no, she's going jogging in a few.

"Beat," I say, tapping a marker on my desk. "Mind if I join? I can climb inside that enormous sweater and hang on for the ride. I could really use some air."

She laughs, holding the mass of wool in her long, elegant digits. "No way. This is my favorite sweater, and you'll stretch it all out."

"So much wool," I tease. "Poor extinct sheep. I only have one question: Was it worth it?"

And she's cracking up and I'm all aglow.

Glow little glowworm, glimmer, glimmer.

I laugh and hum and pick up my marker and draw.

Shine little glowworm, shimmer, shimmer.

And yet she has no clue. She's Never-Ending Pending's longest-running practical joke. *Please, sir, I want some more*, my groveling Oliver Twist heart has squeaked out on repeat since the very first day of freshman year. And I've clutched my clandestine love tight to my heart cage like a stolen loaf of bread I'm starving for but am too ashamed to eat.

Zoë and Maya, my bestest Jacks, think I'm the lone wolf, an island of one. But my constant and unrelenting love orbits me like a distant star. Impossible, unreachable. An infinity of unrequited solitude. And Ms. Hayes, she's in it for the long haul with some zero in a photograph pinned to the bulletin board, his hairy digits gripping the wheel of a sailboat like he's master and commander of all he surveys. Which is flip, seeing as *I'm* the one soaking wet with her. But they're in "love," in Happily Never After, an out-of-bounds, full-daylight, forever variety I've never known, and probably never will. God willing.

It's like I always say, in love, there are two ways to fall apart, two ways to lose your mind and sully your soul. Never-Ending Pending and Happily Never After. I just can't decide which is the harsher ride.

Ms. Hayes sneezes and then laughs and I'm nearly

overcome and I gotta get my hands on that enormous god-damn sweater.

I fake a shiver, I start to chatter my teeth.

"It's subarctic in this cave of yours, Hayes," I say and she cocks an eyebrow. I tremble and quake, shimmy and shake, pumping my arms, and she sighs, knowing all too well what I'm after. Another second or two of my histrionics do the trick and she's peeling the wooly prize from her elegant, slender shoulders. "You're too good to me." I grin as I teeter my desk forward on its front legs and reach to snag it from her hands. She rolls her eyes, bending again to her work, and I push my arms into the enormous bulk of warm fleece and engulf myself in its depths.

And her smell.

And I'm set adrift, I'm out to sea. She is shore and I am ship and her magnificent cliffs rupture my hull and I'm filling with water. I'm half up, half down. Half in, half out. I crash and crash against her. And I sink. Glug, glug, glug.

I take a deep, Ms. Hayes–scented breath, and try to focus back on the poster I'm currently slaving away over, a tragic depiction of Romeo and Juliet, just after he knocks back the poison and she axes herself in the ribs. All those Capulets and Montagues stand around sobbing, staring at the two dead bodies, wishing they hadn't been such crank scat-brains in forbidding the illicit duo. As Ms. Hayes's teacher's assistant extraordinaire, I'm hoping our students will go total Ophelia for all the blood and gore, and maybe even think Shakespeare's the switch for half a second. Maybe.

I grimace, squirming in my seat as an unexpected muscle cramp wrenches in my gut, just over my right hip bone. It bends me over my desk and I instantly regret that third ice cream sandwich I insisted on scarfing at lunch. I tense and feel small trickles of sweat drip inside my armpits, down the backs of my legs. I wait it out, suffering stoically in silence, until it finally releases and I can gingerly pull myself back up. Ms. Hayes is miles away, massively unaware.

I eyeball a pile of photos at the edge of her cluttered desk and slide the stack off, only to be greeted by a bright pair of baby blues, sparkling rainbows, enormous ivory teeth glowing obscenely from ear to big ear. Nate Gray. Our class' perpetual, non-controversial headline, everyday, every-guy, average hit hero. Who also happens to have found Willy Wonka's Golden Ticket to every good girl's panties in town. For the last two years, that good girl's been Eve Brooks, who also happens to be my ex-best, long-forgotten bosom buddy from the middle school days of yore.

"Ugh," I say, fake-barfing in my mouth, flipping to the next shot of Nate, leaning seductively into the grandeur of Ye Ole Sycamore Tree. Then, spread out on a virginal, white draped sheet with his three-thousand-dollar electric guitar and half-lidded bedroom eyes. And last, here's our guy, posing like a prostrate donkey in the middle of an overgrown meadow and at least this one's on-theme, though some circling flies and a pile of steaming dung would really seal the deal.

"So, what," I say, interrupting her again, slapping the photos back down on her desk, "you gonna blow these up and frame 'em? Mount them over your desk for all the world to enjoy?"

She doesn't look up. "Think I should?"

I scowl. "Um, no?"

She shrugs, ever the diplomat. "He brought them by. I think it's sweet," and I can imagine him *bringing* them by, flirting her up with his TV-sitcom haircut and overdriven, oversexed, testosterone-fueled ego, and she, reveling in the unmasked attention, feeling young and sexy and massive ace. Which she obviously is, though I can't tell her that.

"Sweet?" I say. "Nate Gray? *Sweet?* Oh, I know. Like when your cat pukes on your pillow 'cause it missed you when you were gone. Or a pug dog dry-humps your leg 'cause he really, *really* likes you—that kind of sweet?"

"*Lu,*" she scolds, but she's laughing on the inside, I can tell.

"Don't be fooled," I say. "That Jack's a phony. Tried and true. A slithering snake."

"I appreciate your prudence," she humors. "Wise words."

And I slump back, digging a fist into the vise-gripping agony that has suddenly beset my abdomen, another cramp building in the tender depths of my run-amok guts. Goddamn frozen milky confections.

I frown down at my poster, a bitter little pill, barely able to admit that what I'm really steamed about is that it's all too clear who I'll never be. I'll never be Nathan Gray. I'll never flirt up Ms. Hayes. I'll never charm her pants off and she'll wish she were younger so she could flirt right back. I'll never be anything but me and my love will forever be wide of the mark, an unseen Icarus ever soaring to my imminent demise, like a moth to a blowtorch, my wax and feather wings flame and melt and char.

I'm a bobbleheaded, green-eyed monster and I wanna devour Nate Gray whole.

Crunch crunch crunch.

Ms. Hayes goes back to grading her papers, and I wanna make her feel young and sexy. But I never will. I'll just keep breaking my crank heart all over her, for forever and ever and a day. For this is Never-Ending Pending Love.

Welcome to hell. I'll be here all night.

That's when I feel another gripping cramp. And a wet slime emerging between my legs and I squirm in my seat to stealthily slip a finger down my pants, between my legs. Oh dearsweetgeezus no. I roll a marker off my desk and slip my head down to pick it up only to confirm the awfulest of truths—I've gone all period and gore in my pants, bleeding through my black skinnies and onto the pristine white wool of Ms. Hayes's enormous goddamn sweater.

Somebody, please, just ax me now.

<hr>

Ms. Hayes calls after me as I scoot so fast from her room, tail between my legs, sweater mashed into a bundle of yarn under my arm, and I only pray she didn't see the blood.

In the betties' bathroom mirror, my sad-sack reflection sighs as I hold the sweater over the bathroom sink and stare, devastated, into the slick-red fabric of Ms. Hayes's single most prized possession. I turn on the water and watch as horror-flick streams of red run from the wool, over my skin, and into the drain and I just don't think I can ever look her in the eyes again.

My pulse quickens. The water isn't working, and I'm afraid it's gonna set the stain. But I don't wanna use soap 'cause it could ruin the wool.

I wish I were dead.

I cut the water and the orange-brown six-inch blush of bodily fluid is a scarlet letter of shame on my heart. Sweater in hand, I dodge into the bathroom stall and my underpants resemble a battle scene, Massacre at Wounded Pride. I sop up the mess and plug up with some mashed wads of toilet paper and lean my pounding forehead against the cool of the stall wall, deep-down buried in the muck and mire of the latest episode of *Lucy Butler Blows Chunks at Life*.

I sigh, count to one hundred. Do it again. I'm working up to facing the total mortification of the betrayal my uterus has committed, when I hear this small shuffling sound from one of the seemingly empty stalls at the other end of the bathroom. And then it goes quiet. I wait, one, two, three pounding heartbeats. I tell myself it was nothing, willing everyone and everything to just disappear, leave me the flip alone.

I close my eyes again and my mind tangents to eighth grade, when me and some flap-Jacks tortured this poor betty who'd locked herself in a stall after school. *Bathroom Troll, Bathroom Troll, come out, come out, whoever you are!* we sang, camping outside for an hour, laughing through the grate. Turns out her mom was massive sick and we were torturous, psychopathic beasts. I realize now that I'm the Bathroom Troll, hiding out in here for geezusthelord knows how long. It's pathetic. I pull up my pants and stand, pushing open the stall door, and in a moment of time so thick it moves like putty, I look up and come face-to-face with a betty I know too well. I can hardly believe who it is.

She goes still as stone, eyes locked in a vise grip on mine, and I notice a small, white spatula-shaped piece of plastic poised in her hand. And I know those things all too well, from when Marta, my older sister-Jack, used to leave them lying around our shared bathroom at home, giving Dad a coronary every time he took out the trash. My jaw slams to the floor in registering the home pregnancy test as

I stare and stare at none other than the reigning priestess of the perfection personified Pretty Pennies, Miss Evelyn Brooks—aka my ex-best, long-forgotten bosom buddy from the middle school days of yore.

"Eve," I hear someone say, realize it's me.

She doesn't move.

I watch her watching me, shoulders rigid, face tight with fear. Ours is an age-old tale of two betties, apple-Jacks forever, when suddenly one goes ace gorgeous and then, naturally, massive popular. Said popular betty ditches other unsaid, unpopular betty for superhit cool crowd. Girls don't speak again for four years, until a chance meeting reunites them while they await together the results of an underage preg exam. A true, time-honored classic.

Eve gawks, owl eyes wide.

"Lu," she finally says. "It's you. I thought . . ."

I remember Hayes's sullied sweater in my hand and quickly stash it behind my back. I awkwardly thrust a hand in my pocket, jingling away at my keys.

"Word," I say. "It's me." I stand there, jingle-bell-jingling. We both glance back at the test and I quit with the keys. She sighs and my heart goes to sillyputty. "Clash," I whisper.

"Word," she says. "*Massive* clash."

I step back and then to the side. I open my mouth and close it. "Um. This is sorta crickets. I should go. You wanna be solo." But I don't leave. I can't. Plus I still have this whole menses-on-wool situation to deal with. But Eve is watching me. "Okay, yeah." I turn and her hand darts out, grabbing my wrist. My heart stops, skips, putters back to life.

"Stay?"

So I do. And we're hush, waiting, watching for that magical minus symbol, coveted by terrified teenage betties worldwide, to appear. A light blue tint of color seeps into the small window, shimmers, disappears. Eve shakes her head slowly, side to side.

"Nate?" I croak out the obvious, and she nods. "I was just looking at his senior portraits." She frowns and I will the ensuing word vomit back into my mouth. "Yeah, that sounds weird. Never mind. Anyway, you sure it's him?" And she nods again. "Word. I guess I was just holding out hope it was someone else. Like maybe a convicted criminal, or a born-again Bible-thumping preacher-man." She looks shell-shocked, confused. I lace up my fly trap.

My hands fall to my sides and Eve notices the sweater.

"What's the deal?" she asks, her voice tight and thin. "You murder someone in that thing?"

"Um, yeah," I laugh nervously. "Pretty much." I toss it despairingly into the sink. "Basically, I'm disgusting. And massively screwed. It isn't mine."

She laughs and it echoes against the icy white walls.

"You think that's riot?" I say. She just shrugs. "Word," I say, "Well I think—"

But she cuts me off, taking the wooly carnage from me

and laying it over her arm. "Mellow." She takes my hand. "I can fix it."

"No, gimme!" I protest, but she's already pulling me out the door and we're padding down the hall and busting into the nurse's cubicle, two hot-handed crooks, and in the dark dim of cots and cabinets and pills, Eve unearths a tall brown plastic container. I'm cracking up massive at how bizarre this whole situation is, when we're sneaking it back into the betties' bathroom and I'm nearly keeling over when she dumps a mother lode of the stuff onto the wool. But then it starts to bubbling and frothing and I have a feeling that something supernatural is under way.

Eve slowly studies the stain and I secretly examine the slow curve of her swan-song neck. I silently spell her name in my head, E-V-E-(space)-B-R-O-O-K-S. Cool water in my mouth.

Then she hands me the prego pop quiz and I peer down at the test, window still a blank.

"So, you peed on this, yeah?" And Eve shoots me a look, her chin-length amber curls bobbing as she scrubs the wooly blush of my blood with her two bare hands. "I can live with that."

She pushes the sweater back under the tap and the brown bubble-froth foam washes slowly away and down the drain. She cuts the water and I lean in to look and it's like it all never happened. It's like it was never there.

"Holy magic," I say, and she's laying the clean article

out on the counter for us to admire, which we do. Until we stop and stare down at the still-blank prego test in my hand. Cue uncomfortable silence.

"Um," I say. "Thanks."

"Word."

"So."

"Yeah."

"Yeah."

". . . Oh." Her voice wavers and she clears her throat. "I heard you got a full ride for track." And I nod. "That's beat. For throwing the java, um. The jala-vin?"

"That doesn't sound right."

She frowns. "No."

I study her face, and then the test, and then her face. She's stunning. She's as I remember her. She's the most ace betty in our school. Her eye makeup is cloudy, like she's been crying. But this blurry memento of anguish only heightens her abundant appeal as I fight every fiber compelling me to envelop her in my arms and gently squeeze the sweet, citrus sorrow from her lovely, delicate bones.

Eve's lips twitch as a hazy blue line appears, at first faint, and then bold and straight as an ocean horizon. She inhales and I lean in. Verdict: unfertilized! Eve Brooks is not implanted with Nate Gray's lowlife, underage seed! Hallelujahpraisethelord.

I issue a short, echoing laugh and Eve's face softens to a small, lovely smile, the test in her hand falling heavy to her side. I whistle, slapping my mitt on the sink as she stoops to slide the test and box deep into her purse.

"Holy. Crank," I say.

She looks up. "Holy. *Massive.* Crank." And we're laughing, until we're not and then it's sort of crickets.

I feel the oxygen circulating again through my limbs, but see Eve isn't recovering quite as quick. The corners of her mouth are turned down. And I'm desperate for that smile again.

"When I heard you in the stall and I had blood and guts all over myself, it's like I was Bathroom Troll reincarnate," I say. "Remember? *Come out, come out, whoever you are!* You were there."

She nods. "I was so flip over that. You flap-Jacks were so clash to that poor girl."

"Truer words," I laugh, and she smiles, a light blush of color coming to her cheeks. She opens her mouth to say something but then the door is swinging open. And speaking of lowlife, underage seed, here comes Nate Gray's perfect floating head peering around the edge. He sees me and grins. I show my teeth.

"Hey, babe," he says to Eve, voice loud, sugar dripping from the curled-up corners of his slippery lips. "What're you ace ladies up to, anyways? Talking about periods? Or me?" Eve looks at me and our eyes go wide.

"You, Gray," I say, stifling a laugh. "Always you. What else is there?" and he grins, looks convinced.

"We weren't talking about anything," Eve says, pulling her lips tight as she yanks the strap of her bag over her shoulder. She looks in the mirror, dragging the tip of her finger under her eye, wiping away the small charcoal smudge I'd been admiring and I realize that if I admit to myself how much I want her, this ghost from my past, it's likely I'll go insane. So, instead, I robotically wash my hands and stare into the water as they lather like it's the most fascinating thing I've ever seen.

"*Clash*," Nate hisses as he feverishly scans a new buzz. "You clash cog!"

I eyeball Eve. "Crick-ets," I whisper softly and she laughs a teeny tiny bit and I wonder what it would be like to make her laugh all the time. Like as a full-time gig.

"Eve, babe, let's go!" Nate blurts, then closes his eyes, bringing it down a notch. "You look ace, obviously. But we're way tardy and I still gotta drop you off. My apple-Jacks are gonna ream me *hard* a new one."

"Better hustle," I say. "Wouldn't want him to miss out."

Nate smirks. "Ha, ha, Lucy Butler. I'm massive gay and like it up the butt. *So* riot."

I'm surprised he knows my name.

"Okay," Eve says. "Be easy. Both of you." But she's smiling at me sidelong as she slides on peach-scented lip gloss. She steals another glance at Nate, sees he's gone mentally MIA again, and leans over. I breathe her in. "Lu," she whispers, puckering and pursing her newly shining lips.

"For real, that thing we were just talking about, y'know ... the test?"

"Don't mention it," I say. "I won't."

She lets out a gust of fruit-fragrant air. "Switch." She full-swing smiles, her sweet, sad eyes POW! WAM! ZAP!-ing me in the mirror. Holy infatuation, Catwoman. "Good luck," she says. "With the, um, laundry. Stick it under the hand dryer for two shakes and it'll be good as new."

I open my mouth but there's nothing, hot air.

"'Kay, babe," she chirps to Nate, straightening up and crunching a handful of ginger curls in her hand. "Let's jet," and she drops her makeup into her bag. She glances up at me again and her mouth is a small crescent moon. "Thanks," she whispers, grabbing my wrist, and then she's gone.

History

I slow-dissolve the whole ordeal in my mind as I heel it back to Ms. Hayes. In her room, everything smells the same, looks the same, feels the same. Of course it does. But something's different. I hand her back her sweater and she puts it on and it's three o'clock and then I leave. Just like that.

I heel it across the nearly empty student parking lot to my banger and visions of an alternative reality dance through my mind. Eve: dog-tired and greasy-haired, a roly-poly pukester perched on her chest. Nate Gray: beer-bellied and goateed, distractedly pushing a stroller with one hand as the other buzzes his flap-Jacks homoerotic come-ons in dude-bro jargon. Man-o, that betty got lucky with that negative.

I stand beside my banger and press redial on my speak. I've been trying to reach University Bloody Admissions all day. "Thank you for holding," Robo-Cog singsongs. "An agent will be with you shortly."

"Flipit," I say and slam it shut. College is chewing me an ulcer and I haven't even started yet.

I slide into my banger and stew in the wet, stale air. I think about Eve Brooks and I cook in the new, moist oven of an impending heartache. *Not this time*, I think. *Not with Evelyn Goddamn Brooks*. And I push her sad, wonderful mug from my mind, trying to protect the last feeble shreds of this quivering mass of muscle I call my heart. Eve Brooks—she's too taken. She's too straight. She's long gone. She's History.

Ms. Hayes? Ms. Hayes who?

Sailors & Cowboys

It's pouring, so I decide to take a walk. Think maybe a pack or two or twenty of tars will clear my fog-machine mind.

I slip into my rubber knee-high boots, and pull on my raincoat with the smiley-faced whales on the inside liner. I snag my blue knit sailor's cap from my bag, an old seaman's beanie that's slowly fusing to my hair from overwear. I've been sporting this damn thing all winter, cock-eyed and sly, and I pop the collar of my shirts and coats like some secret-agent mystery man. Man-o, I'm so cool, I make ice jealous.

I pull my hood up, and with my head down and my mitts in my pockets, I stalk into the cold foggy face of spring streets, *my witness the empty sky.* As I walk, I count in my mind the one hundred and ninety-four steps up the hill and around the corner to where I can pop off the road and down into the soggy-bottomed woods, where I know Dad or my wee brother, Miles, won't drive or bike by me and throw a conniption fit.

My boots slurp through the melt and muck on the trail and I blaze like a smoldering smokestack. I think about everything, I think about Eve. I think about nothing, I think about Eve. I realize I still have her digits memorized from when we were tiny tykes and I wonder if I could ever just call. Just pick up my phone and dial. Talk for hours about nothing, like we used to.

I drag and think about sailors. Beat sailors on big, old, rusty boats that catch slick fish with thick-roped nets that require endless mending. I imagine I look like a sailor. I hold my lit tar between my lips, and inhale like the Marlboro Man, squinting as the smoke singes my eyes and fills the corners of my hood. I rub together my cold red mitts and think of the sailors rubbing together their cold red mitts just before tying massive, twined knots of figure eights and loops and twists, the freezing, pelting rain ricocheting off their rubber hats. I think I would make a kill sailor. That, or a cowboy.

I mull over the wee tykes in Ms. Hayes's freshie English class and how in school, I'm role-model teacher's assistant and I strut my stuff, presenting well the myth I know who I am. The cast of characters is the same as it was in my day; there's the class badrat, pulling a 'tude and talking back to earn the only attention she's ever gonna get; the jester, first to the punch so that his crank attendance and slipping grades aren't; the shy betty crushing on me, just as hard as I do on Ms. Hayes; and the class flap-Jack, shouting come-ons to me in mezzo-soprano tones to prove he's a big boy in front of his little buds.

I know if any of these wee-Jacks could see me now, they'd start dragging tars—if they haven't already. I remember. That was me. Though don't get me wrong—99.9 percent of me is massive repulsed by the whole crank deal and I hope they never get the nic itch. I've seen the pictures of blackened lungs, the videos of skin-and-bone elders, wheezing through an artificial larynx. Dr. Mom made sure her three children were sufficiently tobacco-traumatized as kids—that is, before she played out her vanishing act, in her wake instructing us in the mysterious merits of abandoning your brood.

All I know is, I hate myself for smoking so much. And if I ever start kissing anyone again I'll quit in an instant. This I know is truth.

Over the river and through the woods, I drag my way through four sticks and at last schlep it across the old, potholed Murphy Farm field and back onto our street. As I'm loping numbly down the hill, Dad comes rumbling up in his truck and thank geezuschrist I'm not still dragging a tar. I pop a piece of gum in my mouth and go to the window.

"Louie, I haven't seen you in days," he says, voice husky from a long day bossing Jacks around in the hospital. His stubble is a gritty shadow on his face and the lines around his eyes are deep, tinted purple. "You okay?" He's a trauma surgeon in the ER and works crazy hours, and whenever he asks me if I'm okay, I have the feeling he'd rather be taking my blood pressure or white blood cell count than actually talking about how I feel.

I nod. "Swell."

He sighs. "I'm off to the market. Emergency cookies and milk run for your brother's Earth Scouts in Technology meeting tomorrow." I roll my eyes and he smiles. "Wanna come, stranger? Be good to catch up."

I imagine us driving into the fog, him rambling about work or my elderly Oma's innumerable health concerns, or Miles, my younger, genius brother-Jack, and his enormous goddamn brain. Or worse, the airwaves will fall dead and we'll cut a wheel in silence, the awkward hush choking our throats, words, like gas, combusted and lost, evaporating and clogging the fragile crank ozone. The ice caps will melt and polar bears'll slip tragically through sharp, gaping cracks into the arctic sea . . .

"Louie?"

I snap into it. "Oh. No. I'm beat."

Y'know, to save the polar bears and all.

"You sure you're okay?" he says, thick eyebrows stern across his forehead. "You're not high, are you?" And I just laugh, walk away. He puts the truck in gear and waves, gunning the gas as I turn to watch his taillights glow smaller and smaller still.

A shivering shambles, I climb the back stairs and stomp onto the porch. I stayed out in the cold rain way too long and I'm a soaking-wet frigid village idiot. Popsicle in Boots. I tromp upstairs and twist shower knobs and pull the sopping layers of fabric from my red-turning-blue skin and shake my arms and pump my fists to warm my ice-cube core.

Warning: Frost Heave.

The water hits my face, chest, arms, in a singeing blast, so hot it feels cold. Glacial streams run from freezing cords of hair plastered down my back and my toes are red-hot roots screaming mercy. My chattering subsides and I'm no longer thaw, I'm simmer. I boil and take mouthfuls of steaming water that warm my ice-cube teeth. My bangs stick in hot slices to my forehead. And my skin tingles back to life.

I close my eyes and think of what a strange day it's been, what a strange world it always is. And then, because it can't be helped, I'm on the trail of Evelyn Brooks like hounds on a fox. So heartbreaking with that smudge of black eyeliner shadowing her golden, freckled face. And her hand on my wrist. And the heat it left, and how warm it was.

My fingers travel over hip bone ridges, lower stomach, and down between my thighs. Pink streams of period wash down me, swirling about my feet, and Eve is checking her makeup in the mirror, peeking at me from the corner of her eye, a small smile curling the edges of her full strawberry lips. I wanna tell her how stunning she is. Show her. Like this. Like this.

But she's a moving target, going backward. She's Ancient History.

But she's right here, and I want to tell her. Like this.

And her mouth opens wide and she's laughing, her pearly whites shining in a Cheshire cat grin. And then Nate Gray is loping eagerly in, a sneaky, slithering snake, pulling her by her waist, cackling head back, teeth bare. The door swings shut. And I'm a blank screen, dead air, white noise.

I open my eyes and am crushed. My hands fall to my water-streaming sides and I have the impulse to put my fist through the fogged-up glass of the shower door. The hot calm the contact would bring, the mess, the glass, the pain. It's just a thought, passing like a storm cloud through my mind.

This kind of misery is the stuff suicide notes scrawled into shower-curtain mist are made of: "Too lonely. Drowned in inch of shampoo water. For best results, rinse, and repeat. I hereby leave my Zippo collection to Zoë Stone . . ."

I slouch against the tile and let the water hit my head and run over my ears in a loud streaming rush until I'm numb.

Pack of Strays

After my shower, I climb into bed naked as the day I was born, a nap-that-spans-infinity on my woe-weary mind. Instantly, my speak buzzes to life.

"Butler," Zoë says. "What's beat?"

"In-n-out," I mumble.

"How did throwing pointy sticks and running in circles go?"

"Track? Canceled due to rainage."

"Word. So, pick you up in an hour?"

I grumble, "Dunno, Zo. I'm hacked, massive."

"Gay."

I sigh. "Jack—"

"Unacceptable, human," Robo-Zoë says. "Pre-evening activities will officially commence in T-minus thirty minutes."

"You get cooler every time you talk like that."

"Obviously," she deadpans. "Now get your butt in gear, flippity-flap. Box chain dynasty dining waits for no man."

I groan and we hang up. I mentally assemble an outfit, which is much simpler than actually getting dressed. I'd forgotten that it's Thursday, aka Betties' Night Out, starring the usual suspects—Zoë, Maya, and me. I'm pondering who this *me* character might be, without much success, when a threatening buzz arrives.

Get ur ass outta bed or we're U-Hauling ur sad sack by the teats into Zoë's whip if it's the last mortal thing we ever do. Clothes, or no.

It's like that?

Believe.

So I lift my *sad sack* from the warm damp of my sheets, take a fistful of pain meds, pull on my visualized outfit, and even push my shag around under the blow dryer a bit. We go out for dinner at the cheapy chain restaurant with the cute waiter Maya always flirts up, and we sneak sips of peach schnapps from a stainless steel canteen called the

Five-Fingered Flask that I pinched from a convenience store many moons ago.

After a few rounds, I find my stride. Here, with these betties, I'm Queen Badrat and I'm up to no good and visions of Eve Brooks fade into the diner's faux-wood facade and knickknack trinkets strung along the walls. I'm superfreeze fly in my patterned button-up and cock-eyed navy hat and I'm one shady character with a big, sideways grin.

"Maya-Jack," I say. "Give Waiter-Shaver a sneak peek of your new PG-13 tramp stamp and he'll think you're so switch he'll finally ask what you're into tonight."

Zoë scowls as she pulls last sip from Five-Fingered. "*Or,*" she says. "Slip him your fake and order Mama some more happy sauce."

I'm in rare form. Medium rare. "*Or,* flash him the Marilyns and you, my dear, can have it all."

Maya spits her water back into her glass, blushing like a 1950s hemorrhoid cream commercial spokeswoman. Zoë pounds her fist on the table—she loves when I call Maya's breasts by their proper name.

"Lu," Zoë says. "I'll show you *my* tits if you give me Five-Fingered."

"Whoa, Jack. Go Children Slow. You can offer to show me your crank water-bra bumps a million times, but you'll never get this flask. I risked my life for this thing. I'm practically an outlaw." I grin, hold up Five-Fingered with one mitt and a peace sign with the other. "Mine-not-yours."

As we heel it out, Zoë and I secretly scratch Maya's name and number on the back of the check, tell him to buzz and we'll whisk him away from his mortal hell in the Flaming Chariot of Fire, aka Zoë's hot whip. But Waiter-Shaver doesn't buzz and we don't say a thing.

We linger in the lot to drag tars and then climb into the Chariot, pour more schnapps into Five-Fingered, and cut a wheel to the club to slice it up. Into the wee hours of night we go mega robo-teckto on the floor, our blood thumping in time with thick, pulsating electro-switch beats. I grind my pelvis into slick-rick shavers all night and even manage to sneak off and talk up the sexy-betty bartender a bit. And, per usual, I'm glad I let my Jacks drag my sad sack out. I'd never tell them as much, but I'm pretty sure they know.

On the late-night drive home, Zo and My sit in the front, scatting up a goddamn gossip storm and I'm sauced and loose in the back, fighting the urge to spill my Never-Ending Pending soul to my apple-Jacks. But instead, I zone out, watching them laugh and wondering where we'll be in two months, ten years, a lifetime.

Us three cats have been apple-Jacks forever, our small group the broken remnants of a larger clan eroded away over the years, school's high tide wishing and washing Jacks in-n-out with the moon. Freshman year, after Eve Brooks ditched my sorry behind for shinier, more glamorous shores, the three of us crystallized into this gang of mis-matched socks. These betties know almost everything about me. Almost.

I catch Zoë's eye in the rearview and she pulls a face, faking like Maya's boring her with prom speak when I know Zo's just as hyped as the next flap-Jack. I think on how much I'm gonna miss them both. Don't know what I'll do without them.

Zoë and I are partners in crime. A terrible twosome. Boris and Natasha, Cheech and Chong, Thelma and Louise without the scarves and skirts. Zoë's a tough nut, hard as rocks, stiff as a board, straight as a nail. Her mom's a drop-out and her dad's a hillbilly hick. She makes it with flap-Jacks in the city—gutter-mouthed Jacks who bartend, and rough, slick shavers who sauce up and work on whips and enlist in the Service. We got mixed up on alters a year back, rolling too hard for too long, totally strung out. Bad news bears and near disaster. But we're on the wagon with the hardgoods. She's superfreeze on the dance floor and riot as hell. She's my closest ally. My rock. Zoë's Tabby Cat.

Maya opens her eyes wide, eating it up, as Zoë inter-rupts to spill on some detail of the particular shape and contour of some unfortunate shaver's nether parts.

Maya, she's way into heart-Jacks. She's henna-dyed red-head, sly, mysterious, awkward, and demure. She's Wife-in-Training and she wears her bleeding heart oozing and dripping onto her perfect sleeve. Clash-Jacks pick on her, shavers especially, who feel her need and desire and use it to wound her. Maya's a good listener and a hornet's nest of honey. Maya's Siamese Cat.

I flip open my Zippo on my pants, over and over, watching the last dim lights of the city fade as we cruise home to the burbs, thinking on what it'd be like to pull a U-ey and speed away from the familiar treetops and ramshackle old farmhouses, plastic-sided McMansions cluttering wide-paved cul-de-sacs. Don't look back, never look back.

Me, I wish I were Tom Cat, but I'm not. I'm Feral. I'm private and elusive, wild and unpredictable. Lone. I'm quick and gritty and keep my scrappy nest of secrets in a den under an old, rusty junk banger. Houdini-junkyard-hobo, that's me.

Together, we're Tabby, Siamese, and Feral. We're a pack of strays and as we pull off and into a twenty-four-hour Quik Stop, Zoë points at the machines, a cuppa joe on her mind; Maya cranes her neck to scope a group of shaver Jacks lingering by the gas pumps; and I have my eye on an ad for a carton of tars inside the store. We get out, go our separate ways without saying a word.

We are feline. Hear us meow.

Ancient History

I can hardly believe track season's over in two weeks when Coach announces it in the quiet, tense moments before our meet begins. Last season ever, for me.

We do team cheer, stretch, and then break, dispersing to our corners to jump and parade around like possessed mechanical monkeys. I'm having (another) one of those days where sex is literally the only thing I can think about.

Javelin in hand, I try and focus my thoughts, step out the distance from start line to launch. I jog, sidestep, mime a throw. My foot goes over the line. I sigh, backtrack, take a look around, watch the 100-meter dashers lugging their blocks across the track, scoping out the competition. I get stuck on a massive ace cornrowed betty, long legs for miles bending into her starting squat. She powers her legs, up and down, up and down, and I try and keep my jaw from grazing the freshly mown lawn.

I know I should be more focused, setting a proper example and everything. I am, after all, co-captain this year, along with my hit-Jack, Luke Castle, the team's star mile-runner, and a betty we all call Rabbit, for her Energizer-like, marathon-style masochism. Together, the three of us are tri-captains. For the past two months I've been tri-ing to care.

I look around for Dad and my wee-Jack brother, Miles—Dad said they might make it—but to no avail. Then Castle saunters by and shoots me a movie-star smirk as he helps some cute sophomore betties with the high-jump mats. He flexes his biceps at me and winks when they're not looking and I flex the middle finger of my right hand.

Every day, before practice, Castle and I drag tars at the edge of the student parking lot and we scat about how much everything sucks. *Flip this, flip that.* You know, the uje. Go-Go Captain Rabbit wheels by in her banger, equipment crowding her back seat, and she waggles her digit at us and laughs, though she really does disapprove. Don't get me wrong, I love Rabbit. But she's in-n-out. She isn't one of us, one of the slack-stars.

At practice, I've weaseled out of my races. I pass the baton and never look back. I tell Coach I hurt my hip flexor doing the triple jump, which is mostly true.

He says, "Bloody 'ell, Butler. Doesn't mean you can't still throw that javelin. You've got a scholarship on the line!" And I hold up my digits in peace signs.

"Rinse and repeat, Coach," I say. "Rinse and repeat."

I watch Rabbit lap the track for the gajillionth time and I yank the cold metal rod from the grass and curl my wrist, laying the silver shaft across my heart cage. I jog, sidestep, extend, and then hurl the steel up and out over the field. It arches through the air and I stand and admire my skills, thinking again about Eve Brooks, Ms. Ancient History. The javelin lands, sticking with a soft, satisfying swish in the manicured green turf and I have this weird feeling—like maybe she's nearby. Delusional thinking, I believe it's called. Then I'm reminded of when all this non-sense began, this throwing pointy sticks and running in circles.

The Crush That Broke the Camel's Back.

Two words. Raine. Hall.

She was a junior enrolled in ninth-grade French. She was doubling up with Spanish, which she already spoke, *fluently*. Madame thought she walked on water. I'm still not sure she couldn't. Cut class, forgot homework, she got away with murder.

We sat in the back of the room and talked. Raine had long hair and sported tight flared jeans, penny loafers, and hippie shirts. We both drew. We did portraits of each other. She said, "Is my nose really that curved?" and ran her finger along its lioness bridge. I said, "Lemme try again," and grew my shag and wore tight flared jeans, penny loafers, and hippie shirts.

She was hit with my Satan-souled older sister, Marta, and they dragged canna and toasted together back in the day before Marta graduated and went on to achieve absolutely nothing. Raine and I, we talked about heart-Jacks. I despised hers. Raine ran track. She said I should try out.

She threw the javelin. I threw the javelin. She did the long jump. I did the triple. She did the high jump. I was crank at the high jump. I asked her if there was a low jump and she took my head in both hands and laughed and leaped over skyscrapers.

She ran the hurdles. I could only muster the 200-meter sprint. She ran long distances in her sleep. She was Dream Queen Gazelle. I was Princess I Heart You Raine Hall.

Twelfth grade. Today. I still run track, am being paid via college degree to throw a sharp piece of steel, jump three times in a row, and run a relay for 200 meters at a time. Raine came to a meet last season and I could barely look at her. She's the Crush That Broke the Camel's Back and I am a caged bird, perched high on my secrets and shame.

And that's when I see *her* perched on the hill.

Evelyn Brooks. Here. At my meet. I was actually, finally, maybe a little bit right. It's a new sensation.

She's watching, looking slightly confused, standing there in this beat knee-length army coat, arms wrapped tight around her too-small frame. Pretty Penny entourage nowhere in sight. I gawk, shaking off the tight weave of Never-Ending Pending memories slowly suffocating my pulmonaries and I wave and she waves, gives me a crooked-smiled, I-know-it's-random-I'm-here shrug. I'm floored.

The javelin judges mosey past and I stumble over myself getting in line. And I throw like a prince. I even take names in my 200-meter relay. I run hard and sure, and after I sprint by the coaches with their stopwatches, I fold at the waist, mitts on my knees, my smoker's lungs burning, and look to see Eve's small frame as she thumbs-ups and waves once more, heeling it off to the student parking lot.

Castle comes up, shoves a thick shoulder into mine.

"Nice sprint, Jackie Joyner. Didn't know you had it in you."

"I don't."

He pokes me in the ribs and I wiggle, turn around, and pinch his left teat. Even though we made out last year and I pretended it never happened, Castle's still my best shaver-Jack. One of a kind. He socks me lightly in the arm and strides away and it finally hits—like seventeen tons of bricks—that high school's really going to end. And Castle and I won't run track. And Zo and My and I won't see each other every goddamn day. *And* that Eve Brooks just showed up to my track meet and I have no idea why, but I sort of maybe do, but can't believe it's true because that's impossible and I'm brain-cell-challenged for even considering it.

I look again for the small silhouette of her oversized coat, see it fading away. She really was here. Imagine that.

In the flesh

It's only 9:30 in the morning and I can already hear Future Dad reading me the riot act over dinner. That is, if he were ever home for dinner.

Zo and I are in it deep, up to our chins, sitting outside Principal Chandler's office awaiting what can only be described as Judgment Day. We're choking on semi-stifled fits of laughter and I close my eyes to take long, deep breaths, my impish accomplice cracking into rippling giggles again and again. We've been unhinged for a half hour straight, the results of said hysteria landing us here after Mr. Payne uncetemoniously slapped us both with the heavy hand of the law.

"Poor Mithter Payne," I say, because I can't help it and there's something mentally wrong with me. "We really thhouldn't give the guy thuch a hard time."

"Thath perpothterouth," Zoë says. "Of courthe we thould."

And it's all over for us, again. Here's the thing, Mr. Payne is a bona fide lemon. And he's got this lisp. And there we were, sitting in physics, brains oozing from our ears, when he draws the lines of a magnetic field and looks up, all feverish and giddy.

Tho, a male magnet tellth a female magnet that from her backthide, he thinkth theeth repulthive. But from the front . . . he findth her very attractive!

But then nobody's laughing and the poor guy's eyes are bugging from his head.

Don't you underthand? he begs. *He thought thee wath hot thtuff! A real thekthy li'l mama!*

And it couldn't be helped: Zoë and I lost our marbles. It wath the thtupiditht thing anybody'th ever thaid. So we go massive Ophelia with laughter for ten minutes straight, holding the class hostage with our hysteria. When Mr. Payne finally gave us the ax, we detoured our trip to the office by busting into the band room and pilfering these massive, two-foot-tall marching band uniform hats, blue and gold with plastic chin straps and ornate, glittering tassels. We got busted a second time, parading repeatedly past Maya's calc class, by the crotchety old hall monitor Mr. Sproul, and now here we are, sitting in too-small plastic seats outside Principal Chandler's office, trying to lace it up, enormous pillars of school pride perched on our gone-amok heads. I'm gonna miss this so much, it's unhealthy.

"Zoë-Jack," I sigh. "What the flip am I gonna do without you next year?"

She frowns. "Seriously. Who am I gonna hate everyone else with?" And I shake my head.

"Really. You're like, you're like my—"

"Can the after-school special, Jack," she laughs, and I open my mouth but she slaps my jaw shut with her palm. She smiles. "I know."

I sigh, sit back, scope her from the corner of my eye. I knock twice on the side of her towering hat. "I dare you to wear this thing in when she calls you."

"Um."

"And you have to walk in and pretend like it's not there." She considers.

"She might call you in first." And I realize I hadn't thought of that.

"Fine," I say, grinning, fidgeting in my seat. "I'm game."

"Me too."

We sit in silence, waiting, tick-tock, tick-tock, till the door

creaks open and we lean forward in our seats. The antici-
pation is deadly. Chandler coughs. And then grunts Zoë's
name from inside. Zo looks at me, eyes wide.

"You can do this, Jack," I say, "I believe in you." But she's
shaking her head. Chandler grunts again, louder, and I yank
Zoë up by the arm, walk her slowly to the door. "Move it," I
say, pushing her in. "But watch yourself," I whisper. *"Theeth
a real thekthy li'l mama."*

And my bestest apple-Jack is all but pissing her skinnies
as she crosses the threshold to her doom, blue-and-gold
band hat perched crooked and proud upon her head.

For a premed prospect, it's Chandler's opinion my attitude's
gonna need a *serious face-lift, major reconstructive surgery.*
I don't remind her I'm an honors student, aced my AP exams,
and recently received the largest Division 1 women's
track-and-field scholarship of any student-athlete, *ever*,
in the history of the school. Not that athletics will auto-
matically make me a viable future MD but it certainly
doesn't hurt.

I'm mulling over how to get out of the after-school deten-
tion she's issued, when I turn the corner, band hat tucked
under my arm, and am suddenly nose-to-nose with none
other than Ms. Ancient History, Eve Brooks, in the flesh,
walking up to the adjacent door of the guidance counsel-
or's office. She's flush-faced, standing on my toes, and I

stumble back, laughing, grabbing hold of her too-bony shoulders.

"Eve Brooks," I yammer. "I understand stalking me, but this is ridiculous." I feel my neck get hot, remembering her tiny frame huddled at my meet.

She smiles, nods at Chandler's door. "Whaddya in for?" and I hold an invisible pistol to my head, pull the trigger.

"Murder?"

I laugh. "Just too beat for this street."

"Beatstreet, eh? Pretty cool."

"What about you? They finally expelling smart kids for making the rest of us look bad?" And she laughs, but then the door opens and she's called inside and I don't want her to go. "You came to my meet," I say quick, and she smiles again, points to the strangeness that is the marching band hat under my arm. And then she's gone, her tiny body moving like a shadow. Outta sight, but not outta mind.

I pick my heart up off the carpet and heel it back to class, taking my precious time. I can picture it now: Eve smiling and nodding as Guidance Counselor UselessMcNobody babbles and banters college bull and Eve sits, starving, wasting away while the Thickly Settled cogs in charge suck grant money off of her switch SAT stats and don't give two flying cranks that one of their best students is an eating-disorder disappearing act.

"This place is a heap of steaming manure," I say to a glass case full of cobwebbed copper trophies frozen forever in mid-throw. I pick up my pace and make a beeline for the cafeteria, figure it's second breakfast somewhere in the world and I can always count on my gal pal Doris in the kitchen to sneak me a plate of soggy huevos rancheros. I'll shoot the breeze with some freshies and munch a snack for the both of us. For me and Eve.

I like the sound of that. Me and Eve.

Loser Express

I'm heeling it up a steep wooded bank into the clearing of our small town cemetery, tar balanced between my lips. I'm feeling dejected, as Zoë's ditched me to hang out with her city-Jacks this afternoon and, while I declined her invitation to go with, I'm still managing to feel left out.

As I walk, I practice dragging without using my mitts. It's beat when the paper sticks to my lips and hangs in this slick, film noir way. I come to my favorite spot, in the far corner of the cemetery, where a large oak stands and pushes its thick, gnarled arms to the sky. There's a stone bench under the tree's muscled old limbs and I sit, lean back my head, listen to nature's clicking, singing, whispery murmur. The ground under my feet begins to dry as the sun's rays arc through the sky's cloudy canopy. I push my hood off and roll up my sleeves and bathe my white winter-bleached skin. I even pull off my navy knit sailor hat and stuff it in my pocket, flick my tar to the ground, stomping it out with my boot. I lean into the tree—*my* tree—eyes closed to soft spring air, and will the sun to pull the heavy, liquid sadness from my core.

When our (my) beloved, elderly K9, Saxby Meredith-Jones Butler the Third (though she was really only the first), was suddenly hit and killed by a neighbor's car, Marta and I heeled it up here after the traumatic, too-real trip to the vet. Dad was outta town with Miles, so us two betties had to deal with it on our own. The hard glare of surgical lights, the sting-smell of antiseptic, the needle sinking into Saxby's dark blue doggy vein. It was last spring, a mirror day to this one. And Marta and I sat on this very same stone bench and I sobbed and sobbed, sad to my rotten core. Marta sat quietly and it was beat she was there, but part of me wished I could just cry alone.

But then she got all massive philosophical, saying, "It's so flip, Lu, 'cause the last time I came up here that's exactly what I did." And I actually believed she had, though I couldn't imagine what she had been so worked up about. I wanted to ask, but never did.

I haven't felt close to my sister like that since, or really before. She's kind of a deadbeat, when it comes down to acting like a human being.

I'm thinking about her up in her dorm, blazing high I'm sure, wondering if it'd be massive weird if I dialed her up, see what's the beat, when I'm zoomed back into the present, voices cutting through my calm quiet. I freeze where I am against the big tree, careful not to move an inch. I watch as a shaver and betty, hand in hand, heel it along the opposite side of the graveyard, light glinting in shards around the edges of their silhouettes. They go for the obvious spot in front of the view and set up a blanket by the bench over-looking the rooftops and hills of the town below. She's gig-gling and his deep voice comes in short, amused bursts.

I'm invisible. My back morphs into the grooves of the tree and bark crawls up my skin and I watch, unseen, as all trees do. Together, they make the perfect picture-that-comes-in-the-frame-when-you-buy-it couple and the whole thing's just too Hallmark for me to handle. I'm about ready to stand and make my escape when they start get-ting all frisky, swapping spit. They slump back onto the grass and the guy's hand goes sliding up the girl's loose shirt. And then her dainty hand starts working its way over the crotch of his expensively faded and torn jeans and I'm paralyzed, mortified, an animal, caged.

I look to my left, then to my right, plan my getaway in my mind—through the baby graves, under the canopy, over the bramble pile, down the hill. I stand, crouched low, ready myself to bolt, Flash-style, total-stealth. But just as I'm picking my first, tentative steps up and over the gnarled roots of the towering tree, the girl turns her head and she scopes me. I slow to a crawl, suddenly caught in an atmospheric patch as thick as blackstrap molasses, and I watch her eyes squint and then widen as she recognizes me. I recognize her, too, see she's the brown-haired Pretty Penny, one of Eve Brooks's doting minions and besties forevs. I freeze, realizing just how massive Ophelia I must look crouched there, hair all mussed up, rain boots up to my knees, a smiley-faced whale raincoat rolled up to my elbows, just *staring*.

Then the shaver-Jack, caught in the act of pulling his shirt over his head, turns, and I see it's none other than the enigmatic Nate Gray in the flesh—literally. And me, I'm beyond gone and I don't look back. I heel it down the slanting path, slipping on last fall's wet, rotten leaves, hating the flip out of everyone, and all that's wrong in this world, and myself and my crank awkward alwaysness.

"Lucy Butler?" I hear him yell. "What the—?"

And I'm running, chugging along, the back of my throat burning and aching. I fall, get up, fall again.

I am the Loser Express. Choo choo.

I get home, rattled to my core, and see there's a note from the remaining two residents of the Butler abode saying they're out for the night and the place is all mine. There's even money for a pizza. I order delivery, do about ten thousand crunches, three hundred jump ropes, fifty or so (not in a row) legit, flat-backed push-ups. I pump up the tunes in the living room and rattle our McMansion with switch, swashbuckling beats until the grub arrives and I stuff my face and play video games till my eyes go blurry.

I decide I never saw what I saw, and then I decide I did, and I'm gonna tell Eve. She deserves to know, and I'm gonna spill. I sneak sips from a fifth of gin in the cupboard and dance till I'm slick with sweat, honing my skills in the reflection of the porch's darkening double doors. I recover. I bounce back.

I'm gonna call Eve and I'm gonna tell her what's what. And she's gonna cry and ask me to come over, and cry some more in my arms. It's totally maybe gonna happen. It totally maybe could.

I collapse into my bed, an entire small veggie pizza pie shifting around happily inside my gut, thinking about Eve, Ms. Ancient History, with my phone—my six-shooter—lying ready at my side. I recite her digits in my head, and the moments tick by and my heart beats faster, faster still. Until, until, until, I'm running out of steam, the night blanketing down around and over a moment that's fading away. Gone.

I lie in my now-dark room, listening to the quiet,

gurgling murmurs of my digestion, and think about Eve, and how totally Ophelia it would be for me to call her, dish it all. I won't do it. It wouldn't be right.

I pocket my pistol and curl up into a ball, falling asleep with the soft, oval pucker of Eve's strawberry lips lingering on my wayward mind.

Thank You for Holding

I'm cutting a wheel home from my last track meet of the season when Dad buzzes in. I'm feeling pretty good, tunes blaring, dragging a tar. For cheap thrills, I smoke as we talk.

"Hi, stranger. It's Dad." Like I don't know who it is. "How did it go?"

"Eh, we flipped."

"Oh, congrats, kid!"

"No, Dad, we lost." I pull up to a stop sign and exhale a perfect ring out my open window. "We're losers."

"Oh."

"Whatevs. At least the season's over."

"I'm so sorry. Miles's Project Brain meeting ran late." Project Brain, so subtle. "I'm really gonna miss watching you throw," and I can hear him smile, can picture his stubbled mouth creasing at the edges, his head tilting at that angle like I'm still five years old and he forgot it was my birthday—again. "Guess I'll just have to make the trek up north next year and catch a couple of your D1 college meets!" I'm a silent stone. "Anyway, you joining us for dinner tonight? Fried chicken and corn on the cob!"

Miles's favorite. I was planning on heading home, but am not really feeling it now. I chuck my tar out the window and hear Miles, in his pre-pube, nine-year-old vocal stylings, singing in high falsetto to the theme song of their favorite cartoon and then Dad's laughing, talking too loud to him in an unfunny voice.

"I don't think so."

"What, Louie? You're not coming?"

"Yeah, no—" But I'm cut off as he's hollering to Miles. The line goes silent and I yell into the receiver, "Dad? I'm not coming! I'm hanging up!"

He's laughing as he gets back on, as if he's trying to piss me off. "Louie, this is a special night. Your brother's team *won* the Regional Electric Mini Sub Race! And you missed dinner last night, too. Not that anyone's keeping tabs."

"Yeah, and you missed it the night before. And the night before that. Not that anyone's keeping tabs," and he goes quiet, knowing I'm right. "Dad, I just can't. Okay? Be easy. I gotta jet."

"Fine," he says, and I can tell he's hurt.

"Look. I was thinking maybe this weekend we could all go scope that flick at the drive-in. I can't remember the name. The remake of the corny one you mega dug when you were a wee-Jack."

"Oh, Louie," he says, and the regret in his voice makes me fume. "That sounds *so* nice. But we're in the city both days for Miles's—"

"Switch," I say, cutting him off.

"Louie—"

"I don't care."

"Well, you obviously do."

"I obviously don't."

He sighs.

"We'll talk when you get home."

"No, we won't because I'm not . . ." But I can hear he's already beeped off. "Thank you for holding," I say to no one, hanging up.

I wheel past my street and call in a turkey-bacon sub at the sandwich shop, but as I pull into the parking lot, I realize I don't have my wallet. Good thing I'm not post-hibernation hungry and just competed my backside off in a three-hour-long track meet.

I tool around, feeling massive jammed and self-sad, wishing I had something stronger to smoke or perhaps a loaded gun, when I remember the gas card my little Oma slipped me last time I cruised by her house. I pull into Citgo and stock up on dried fruit, orange fishies, and enough beef jerky to feed a small, meat-loving nation. I'm scheming a shiny quarter from the leave-a-penny, take-a-penny when I sense a presence hovering behind me and I turn around and her gaze is a tractor beam searing red-hot into the tender flesh between my eyes.

Oh woe is me.

Amelia Long, class pariah. She focuses her enormous, watery eyes on my own and plasters on a greasy smile. Three months ago I swore I'd never hang with her again. Yet here she is. And me, I got nothing. I got orange fishies.

"Hidey-ho, Amelio," I mumble, not meeting her eyes. I shuffle toward the door, pocketing my quarter and tearing my teeth into the oily wrapper of a Slim Jim. I'm so hungry, my hands are beginning to shake.

"Oh, word, Lu!" she says, squeezing my name from the depths of her self-loathing. I flinch, eyeballing the kid behind the counter, finally place him as one of the quiet freshie-Jacks who sits shyly in the back of Ms. Hayes's freshman English. I feel my face burning apple red as Amelia steps closer, the sweaty heat of her desperation and need vibrating between us.

"Good news," she says, too loud. "I'm clean! No crotch crabs!"

"Yay." I grimace, averting my eyes as another customer jangles through the door.

And I remember all too well the last time Amelia conned me out, maybe four months ago, scheming a free concert and all-you-can-eat alters. Naturally, there was no show, no drugs, just a few empty kegs, a crowd of flap-Jacks I didn't know, and an ingrate of a non-heart-Jack flap-Jack who announced to Amelia she most likely had the creepy-crawlies infesting her nethers. It was freezing cold that night and when I got home I spent a painfully sober hour hosing down and scraping off Amelia's ice-encrusted vodka vomit from the outside of my passenger's side door. Quoth the Raven *Nevermore*.

And I've got one foot out the door when she asks what I'm getting into that night. My too-heavy heart sinks, my mind fast-forwarding to my wide-open itinerary; angry parental simmering at home, a cold bowl of cereal schemed after dark, bestest apple-Jacks gone prom-crazed Ophelia with mani-pedis and spray-on tans. I hesitate too long and Amelia's train is chug-a-lugging off its tracks. She gushes, telling me she's way into some toaster in the city and that they're all scoring a sinkload of E and it's gonna be hecka massive kill and I'm super flip if I miss out on this crazy amazing time. I remind her Zo and I have been on the outs with alters of the fourth power for a year now and then she says Clarissa's gonna be there and was begging her to bring me by.

Clash.

Zoë and I, we call Clarissa Molly Master Jack 'cause she's always holding the bestest, purest, whitest slip. She carries only primo candies and is the funniest damn cat you could ever imagine. She's got this curly red Afro, and she's always standing in the middle of a hundred hit-Jacks telling these stories, like how she thinks about her kitten getting bit by a rabid raccoon and dying whenever she needs to cry at funerals and sad flicks, or how her bestest betty, so-and-so, crapped in bed while doing it with some flap-Jack after snorting snow. Clarissa and her E are massive bad news bears, but she makes me laugh until I cry and I could use a little pick-me-up right about now. Not to mention she's got that pure white slip. I won't tell Zoë, she doesn't have to know. She'd go mental if she found out.

"I . . ." I sigh. "Sure. I'm free. I think. Buzz me the address and I'll meet you there. *Maybe*."

"Switch, Jack!" Amelia grins. "Um, I just gotta swing by my place first. I forgot the address there. I, like, wrote it down."

"You wrote it down."

"Word. Actually, can you give me a ride? I was just gonna

walk back, but it's, like, *really* far." She slippery smiles, and it dawns on me that it's happening again. That it's entirely possible there is no party and no drugs and no Molly Master Jack. It was the drugs! I blame the drugs!

Miserable but resigned, I agree to give her a ride, holding out hope in a hopeless world. It's nice, at least, to have a little company.

We pull in and her house is a massive pit. It's this crank mole hole of an apartment she and her dad, who's never home, have been shacked up in for years, with a billion cats and dogs who are always pissing and yakking brains all over the floor. I flop on her bed as she pretends to look for the address and then I help her clean the kitchen, which is filthier than any kitchen I've ever seen. And then because it's getting late and the "party" falls through and her new litter of kittens are so flipping cute, we cue up a flick and sit under blankets and smile and laugh as three furry-whiskered, munchkin-faced monsters climb and push their tiny, fluffy heads through tunnels of fabric, mewing and generally raising G-rated ruckus.

We're sipping off Amelia's dad's D-Day-sized Miller Lite mega-stash and scoping the trailer for a new action flick, when Amelia laser-locks her watery, probing eyes onto mine. I'm feeling a little loose and am scatting on how some actress—what's-her-name—is, like, totally drop-dead ace to the max, and how if I were a shaver-Jack, I'd wanna snag her. Amelia smiles, her shiny eyelids slack at half-mast. She rubs a clammy-palmed hand on my back and nods her bobblehead up and down.

"Y'know, Lu, that's coolio." Her eyes probing my soul with their stare. "I'm hit, Jack. I got your back."

"Huh?" I say. "Come again?"

She smiles again. "*You* know."

I think I do, but really don't want to. "No," I say, looking away. "I don't."

And Amelia just shrugs, turns back to the TV. "Like . . . whatever," she mumbles. "To each her own. Girls, guys, whatevs."

She trails off, and as the hotter-than-Sahara starlet scampers across the screen in full, superhero getup, I feel my scalp tingle with heat and the crooks of my palms flash with sweat. I pick up the little black kitten with white socks and stick my nose deep into the softest-soft fur behind her ears and suddenly, I think, maybe I'm gonna cry. I hold her there, her warm animal belly like a hot water balloon in the palm of my hand, and two or three hot tears roll from my eyes into the soft, sweet down of her fuzzy, dark fur. I breathe back a swell of fire in my chest, and, thankgeezuschrist, Amelia can't pester me again because her grubby dad shuffles through just then, hollering at us for snagging his sauce, and dumping all over Amelia for not cleaning up after her filthy pride of tiny beasts. He finally leaves, in a huff, and Amelia, unfazed, gets to flapping her mouth, gabbing through most of the credits about this new shaver-Jack she's maybe seeing, like, sort of.

The movie starts and Amelia doesn't shut her trap and, about twenty minutes in, I check my pulse, find it's still on the marathon-racing side of normal, and say I gotta jet. I tell her my allergies are flaring up and Amelia nods miserably and I heel it outta there, nearly sideswiping the three and a half junk bangers crashed out like enormous, metallic corpses on the apartment complex's dirt-and-weed front lawn.

I look back as I shift from reverse into first, and see Amelia's watery, moon eyes peering out from the front door screen. She smiles, holding up a kitten, waving its tiny, fuzzy paw *goodbye*. I wave quickly back, drive on, and think about how good it's gonna feel to get home. Clean, quiet home.

And it does, it really, truly does. I walk in and there's Miles and Dad, curled up on the couch watching a cartoon flick and all the dishes are clean and the lights are low and the carpet isn't jumping with fleas. I slump down next to Dad and he smiles, yanks on one of my braids. I scheme a cookie from Miles's plate and he whines, so I get up, grab a handful more, and we all munch and watch and laugh in easy peace.

Jazzed

At long last, it's prom. All the betties in town are jazzed on sentimental overdrive, torpedoing around like women possessed, in jeans, button-up blouses, and hundred-dollar aerosol-sprayed updos.

"The prom is ruining our environment," I say to Zoë and watch as her gorgeous blond coif is teased and plastered and cajoled around her head like a curlicue helmet. "I think prom was born when Beelzebub, Miss America, and the Tooth Fairy had a three-way and pumped out masses of squealing, teeming, acrylic-nailed bride-princess-zombie spawn." She rolls her eyes and scopes the magazine in her lap. "Prom and I are, like, so not talking."

"Go Children Slow, Jack," she says. "It's truth prom is *massive* gay," and I cringe, look up, see she didn't notice. "But let's be honest. You're just tweaked 'cause you wish you were going."

"I think maybe I'm just depressed." And Zoë sighs, sadness and feelings and hugs being massive outside of her jurisdiction. "No. I just really wish I hadn't let you con me into coming here."

"Nobody begged you."

"Well, yeah, you kind of did."

"Nope. Didn't."

"Yup. Did."

Zoë shakes her head and I stare out the window. This whole pre-prom hysteria week, I've been so checked out, peering through a foggy glass pane at the frenzy and mania. Nothing touches me and sounds are muted and the world zigzags by. I don't have a dress. I don't have a date, an updo, a downdo, bronze skin, or glitter glued to my cheeks. I don't have an orchid to string around my wrist with a scrunchy band that smells like eucalyptus. I don't find I particularly want these things. But my apple-Jacks, along with every other betty on the planet, certainly seem to.

Zoë and Maya work to erode my will all afternoon—over flower pickups, a last-minute, emergency strappy-shoe search, and a pre-prom booze cruise—pestering me to come stag or call up my ex-heart-Jack, Eli. But I manage to resist. They drop me off at home, and I soon find myself back in bed, cozily curled up to a *Dick Van Dyke* marathon and a bowl of O's, the sun setting gently outside my open window.

Just as Dick is tripping over his third peskily situated ottoman, Maya buzzes me a picture of her face frozen in a sulky-eyed pout. Then another, a blurry white confection of lace and taffeta and the words *My ass. Too big!?!?* And I'm laughing so hard I surprise myself when I call up my track buddy co-captain crony, Luke Castle, and tell him he should come with to the dance, say we can make fun of everybody and feel good about how much more awesome we are. I know he'll say yes, too, because he and his short-term betty just called it quits and he's massive on the rebound. As friends, I say, but of course.

"'Cause after all," I wax philosophically to Zoë five minutes later on my cell, "it's prom, once-in-a-lifetime goddamn hell-on-earth prom, and I know if I miss it, I'll kick myself when I'm a hundred and six, fluffy white shag, a half-dozen teeth and as many fond memories left to my name. Y'know?"

"I hate you," she says, but then both she and Maya agree to help me get dressed last minute via video chat and Maya tells me to try on the dress Marta wore a few years back, a jet-black flapper-style number, that shockingly fits like a mitt. I insist on wearing bomber boots and my shag straight down and leave it at that.

I tell my apple-Jacks I love them and we hang up and I sit in my room for an hour, chewing my nails, waiting in my fancy-pants threads to avoid any unnecessary parental or sibling oglings of any kind until the last possible second when I jet the sixty-three steps from bedroom to banger. In my mad dash, I find nobody's home, so it doesn't actually make any difference either way.

Castle and I meet there, no I'll-pick-you-up-at-eight funny stuff—just two hit-Jacks hanging out. He's got a cane and top hat his grandfather used to wear, and one of those black tees with an iron-on cartoon tuxedo, and we look like some kill postmodern Bonnie and Clyde remake. We eat at a table with Zoë, Maya, and their two man-glam dates as they all pull sauce from Five-Fingered like thirsty fools crawling through a desert. I take a few half-hearted swigs while a geriatric DJ starts to spin the hits of yester-year and the century before, the walls lousy with pruney streamers and starry ornaments sagging in the corners. After grease-coated chicken à la factory farms and spar-kling corn syrup cider, slugged back from complimentary *Glam-R-Us* champagne flutes, we disperse.

Castle dances with his Jacks, so I dance with mine. He locks his James Dean laser beam on some flip junior, Kylie Something-or-Other, and spends the beginning of the night cutting in on her and her pimple-mugged date. Kylie is wooed from the poor flap-Jack's scrawny arms and into Castle's throbbing track-star muscles, and he shoots me thumbs-up during a slow number, Kylie draped like a pet monkey around his neck.

At one point, "Girls Just Want to Have Fun" comes on and the betties' track team goes Ophelia. This is our song. Season-long, we warmed up to it and played it max volume on the bus to every meet. We squeeze into a tight group, Rabbit and I in the middle, howling away, and belt the lyrics at the top of our lungs and we own this song, it's only for us. When I return to our table, I overhear Zoë whisper to Maya, "Other Jacks like that song, too," and Maya nods absently while Zoë rolls her eyes. Way crickets. But I cut Zoë some slack because I know she pretends to be annoyed when really she just feels left out. I slip her Five-Fingered and tell her she can hold on to it for the night.

Amelia Long comes over and tries to linger but Zoë and Maya are cold as glaciers and Amelia, after ten minutes of rejection-neglection, miraculously takes a hint and wanders away. I feel sort of bad for her but I also don't want her shuffling around me all night, scatting about how we got real over a movie and kittens, asking me what I'm into after prom.

I act blasé when Diva Eve Brooks, Ms. Ancient History, and her clan of untouchable flap-Jacks with their shavers-in-waiting all arrive late. Eve's chosen for prom queen (gasp!), and Nate, king (boo! hiss!), and Eve smiles and holds her bouquet of red roses to her heart cage in long, elegant fingers. As she heels it by us, I step aside and bow my head.

"Your Lordship," I say, and she looks at me hard.

"Beatstreet Butler." She smiles, sliding one of her dethorned floral adornments into my hand. I break off the stem and push it into my hair and Eve holds my eyes a second longer than I expect. Then Nate comes slithering up, scooping her elbow in his hand.

"What's the switch, Lucy B.? Looking ace as ever!" he says, even though we obviously hate each other, his voice so syrupy sweet it makes my teeth ache. And then the Pretty Pennies plus Entourage are heeling it away in a rowdy group of taffeta and silk, off to some kill toaster we're certainly not invited to. And I can't help but wonder what other prom-court She-Penny that two-timing, scat-for-brains Jack-ass has exchanged the royal fluids with.

I know I gotta tell Eve that Nate cheated. It's what a good person would do, I think, as I watch the blur of stretched limos pulling away beyond the front door before rejoining my dance-fevered Jacks to cut up the floor. But I know I won't.

I'm painfully, though humorously, enduring Maya's theatrical grinding against me from behind—all for her slobbering date's sake, who, Zoë and I agree, has a neck thicker than Jaws's—when I see Castle grabbing his coat and throwing it around Kylie Something-or-Other's twig-thin shoulders. She kisses him on the cheek and runs to her apple-Jacks to say she's leaving with superman mile-sprint-stud Luke Castle. He waits, posing like James Bond by her table. I turn around and pat Maya gently on the top of the head and weave through the sweaty crowd to where he stands.

"Word, Lu," he says. "I'm gonna jetset."

I nod. "You wanna drag tars real quick?" I lean forward, pushing my palms into his granite-solid chest.

"I do."

"I now pronounce us husband and wife," I laugh, and he cocks an eyebrow, gives me his Dirty Harry stare. He heels it over to Kylie, who's trying to pry herself away from her Jacks, and slides his tars from the jacket of his coat still perched on her back. I watch as he explains what he's doing and I see her turn to look at me, the disappointment registering on her pointy mug. You'd think the betty's pet hamster had just escaped and crawled down the washing machine pipe and drowned (true story) by the pout she slathers on. He puts his mitts on her cheeks and I know he's promising they'll jetset soon. Then Castle and I are heeling it outside and the night air is like a cool balm on our sticky skin.

"You look superfreeze in your suit, apple-Jack," I say as he lights it up.

"And you yours." He passes me the tar.

"Man-o," I sigh, and we sit on the curb, the many flaps and fringes of my dress flurrying like black snow to rest limply on my knees. I look at him, watch his face. "It's switch we came tonight. It's been almost actually fun." He nods and drags on his tar. "I'm gonna massive miss your ugly mug next year," I say and lean my head on his shoulder.

"It's been real, it's been good, but it hasn't been real good," he says and then he's rubbing my back and I lift my head to plant a wet one on his cheek and then his lips are on mine and we're kissing. I kiss him back for a second, and then one more second too long, but then am putting my mitts to his heart cage, pushing him away. And he stands, his expression unequivocally *I hate your guts now die.*

"Really, Lu? *You're* pushing *me* away?"

I open my mouth and he turns, ready to heel it away. "Castle, be easy, Jack," I say, standing, my hands raised.

"You flip flapping betty," he says, shaking his head. "Why did you even invite me here tonight? And why did I even come? I should have known you were gonna play some crank Lu Butler stunt tonight. I can't believe I let you sabotage this thing with Kayla—"

I grab his arm, my mouth wide. "Wait." I frown. "Her name's Kayla? I thought it was Kylie."

"Lucy, for real," he says, tossing off my hand. "I need you to back off."

"Castle," I plead. "Listen, I didn't know you were beat for me. I never would have spit-swapped with you if I knew."

He laughs loudly, flicking his tar to the turf. "Oh, well, thank you very much for your thoughtful consideration."

"I really don't know what my problem is," I say. "I'm sorry. I really, really am."

He works at his cheek with his teeth. "Stop being so goddamn sorry for me, Lu," he finally says. "I'm not sorry. I massive liked you, and for that, I'll *never* be sorry. But you? You don't like *anyone*, and *that's* your problem. Nobody's good enough for Lucy Butler. Too effing beat for the entire flipping school." I want to talk, but suddenly I can't. And then he's storming back into the dance, the front doors swinging in his powerful wake. I stand in shock for a minute, until I suddenly feel completely frozen, chilled to the core. I'm shivering, my teeth chattering away. I know he's right. He's totally right, in such a completely wrong way.

I go back inside and the heat-and sweat-drenched air is overwhelming. I find Zoë and Maya and say I'm jetset. They're pulling on mysterious little half shirts and tugging fancy sequined purses over their shoulders and they agree, say we've got plans to get into some sauce after the dance. I say I don't feel good, that I'm hacked, but they both get on me like I'm lamer than ducks. There's some toaster in someone's fancy hotel room, and I say I haven't brought a change of clothes and don't feel like hanging out with a group of mop strangers in my sister's scratchy old prom dress all night.

In the parking lot, my apple-Jacks argue and pull me toward their whips.

"Get in, Grandpa. I'll wheel," Zoë says, pleading with her eyes for me to come.

Maya's less committed. Her date keeps grunting and picking her up by the waist from behind. "Loser Lu," Maya whines as Beef-Neck Man grabs her around the shoulders, practically knocking her off her spiked heels. She pulls away, squealing, and then she's doing this little booty dance, hollering about how her thong is giving her a massive double wedgie.

Beef-Neck grabs his crotch, says, "I got my thong on, too, Jack. Wanna see? It's all about the bulge, baby!"

"Gay!" Zoë yells as Maya delivers a slew of prissy she-slaps to Beef-Neck's arms and pecs.

I laugh half-heartedly as I climb into my banger and Zoë leans onto my windowsill, rolling her eyes as Maya emits another eardrum-rupturing shriek. Zoë's date, Gideon, her on-again, off-again, comes over and puts his hand on her back but is watching the others goof off in the parking lot and I can tell she and him are *so* gonna hook it up tonight. With Maya practically leaping from her dress, and Zoë and Gid as good as gone, I know I'd be the depressive, sauced-up fifth wheel all night, and my ego can't handle another blow.

"This is gonna be kill without you," Zoë says, half smiling. "Thank you for holding, flap-Jack."

"I'm sorry, Zo," I say, my head throbbing. "But I just can't tonight. I'm totally hacked. Massive crank."

"I know, I know," she says. "You're always crank, or hacked, or in-n-out. You're just mega lame, what can I say?" She laughs but I know she's partly serious, because it's partly true. We both watch as Beef-Neck yanks down his pants waist to reveal the straps of a skimpy white jock-thong and Maya gasps, her face going Kool-Aid red. Zoe just shakes her head. "This shaver really actually might be gay. Like, gay gay. Not just like, oh that's so gay. Y'know?"

I shrug and pull my mug into a forced smile. "For real," I say. "Have fun. Stay safe. Rinse and repeat. Use protection. And for scat's sake take care of our sauced and sassy apple-Jack tonight. Resist the urge to gag and chuck her in the trunk." Zoë finally breaks, cracking a grin, and Maya pops her head in between ours. She leans into my banger and kisses me on the cheek.

"Baby Lu, why so blue?" she says, putting her mitt on my mug and sticking out her lower lip in her patented drama queen pout. Even though it's just Maya, it feels nice to have someone touch me.

I shake my head. "I'm just massive wiped, My, that's all. Had a little row with Castle."

"Lover boy," Zoë smirks and Maya smiles, wobbling a little, putting both mitts back on the windowsill.

"Steady, betty," I say, ignoring Zo. "My, let me jetset your sauced ass home," but she stands, suddenly composed, and backs away, smiling and blowing kisses. She stumbles over her heels.

"Go Children Slow there, killer," Zoë says, laughing and grabbing Maya's flailing arm. Zoë looks at me with roller-coaster eyes.

"Thickly Settled," I say, tapping my skull with a digit.

"Drug-Free Zone," Zoë laughs, lugging Maya's arm over her shoulder. I start my chug-a-lug engine and Gideon pops his head into my window. "Be easy, Lu," he says and jogs in front of my wobbly apple-Jacks.

Maya points crookedly at his back. "Ped X-ing," she announces unevenly and we are all cracking up as I pull away.

Driving home, my temples throb and I wonder what's wrong with me, why I can't seem to muster the gumption to get into the end-of-high-school spirit, why I don't like anything, or anybody, particularly myself. I think about Castle's words. I think about Diva Eve, and her sweet, sad eyes, and if she and Nate are doing it now and if Eve thinks it's good. Lost in the shadows of other peoples' lives, I drive home and it takes a thousand years, the soft blossom of Eve's rose pressed to my nose.

I'm woken up late night by my ex, Eli, dialing my speak. Normally I wouldn't answer, but out of sheer loneliness, I scat him for a bit, still half-asleep. He's massive blazed, clogging the airwaves with jive, as he's coming down from magic mushroom mania.

"My hit-Jacks are getting massive into some hydroponic Big Bud tonight and we're gonna push it tomorrow at this festi on the coast. Actually, there're an extra ticket, if you're into it . . ."

I realize I've been summoned to participate and groggily sit up. "Did you just say you're pushing hydroponic Big Bird? Don't you think it's time you Jacks invested in some big boy pot?"

He laughs. "Big Bud—not Bird. And this stuff's massive kill. Smith said it won the Holland Cannabis Cup in like '98 or '99 and we found these skuzzers in the city who grow it in this mega-warehouse. It's that vintage scat."

"Oh, good. Skuzzers. Sounds safe."

Crisis averted, I think, as he's off again, talking in loops about some flick he's scoping on TV I've seen already, about gangsters and hard knocks. I zone out, thinking back to when we were together, cooped up in his dingy TV den every weekend night, him always slinging his heavy old brick of an arm over my shoulder, his fifty-ton muscles lying limp for hours on the delicate tendons and cords of my neck, me terrified that if I moved he'd clobber me with his raging libido.

And when we did fool around, I'd rush through our hot-handed, sweaty-palmed gropes, his enthusiastic forays into female oral enjoyment, and I would grab him and work him, delivering him to that coveted, post-firework place where it was no longer about getting off. And finally, at long last, he'd kiss me slow, his face damp with sweat, his lips so warm and gentle, his desire quiet.

But that was the problem with Eli. You could never just scope a flick or cuddle without getting a headache or giving a hand job.

"Y'know?" he's saying, waiting, so I grunt into the receiver, pick up a half-eaten energy bar on the floor.

His familiar voice lulls me. Equal parts sweet, cute, smart, and just a pinch Ophelia—his laundry list of ingredients should have made for my perfect heart-Jack confection delight. He treated me well, dialed every night, loved being around me, told me I was the most ace betty in the room (he's a good liar, too). But with Eli, I never knew what to say back to him. I just never wanted to give him what he needed.

But I had fun, too. He carried me on his back and we tore around theaters and toasters and suburban streets a-hollering and we'd sauce in the woods with his Jacks and they'd say, "Get a room," when we fell laughing and kissing to the crackly forest floor. And the alters. So very many alters.

Mostly, Eli was fun, I mean, he was into being happy, which is rare. Then he said, *I love you*, and I laughed, said, *Too soon*. I think maybe I broke his heart a little, which kinda breaks mine.

And now he's talking about his prom, how he went with some snowed-out rich-Jack betty from upstate and I wonder if they got a hotel room, like he and I did, at my junior prom, one crazy, long year ago. It was my idea to finally do the deed, and he was gentle and never pressured me at all. But during, it was as if my entire body went numb and my brain completely froze. I mopped out. At one point, I realized my fists were so clenched that I could barely unravel my fingers and they stayed cramped like that for hours. Even now, I feel a little sick just thinking about it.

But you can't say I didn't try.

Eli laughs. "And so I was totally like, 'Word, Jack. Gotta spring for the stretch Humvee—or nada.' Y'know what I'm saying?"

"Mmm," I hum, roll over onto my belly, my eyes pulling shut.

After we had sex, he said, *You went totally coma. When I tried to get close and get under the blankets, you pulled away and cramped up like a cocoon. All night long I was frozen, subzero.*

Yup. That about sums us up. We would just have sex and then I'd crawl away with all the covers and he'd be clueless and freezing to death in his polka-dot boxers. He never would have just put on more clothes, either, or gotten another blanket, or asked me what the deal was. He'd just rip some canna and zone out. That's just who he was. And I was always the crank.

We left each other out in the cold.

I tried, I really did. I even gave the Jack a blow job in those post-breakup days, which was actually not so clash. Not so switch, either. I had always been traumatized by the image of myself bobbing up and down on any shaver, like some unwitting porno star, sleaze-style. But I trusted Eli and made sure we were in total darkness. While I was giving him head, he didn't say too much about it, so as not to pressure me, but I could tell it was one of the most beat things he'd ever had done. And I don't know why, I just didn't really care.

"So, Jack," he's saying now. "I know it's, like, a million o'-clock, but I think it's high time you come over and blast the trees with me and Smith," and I'm half thinking why the flip not, when Maya calls in, and, thank geezuschrist, too, because if I had caved and gone, I never would have gotten him off my back. I can see myself now, cruising to some remote skuzzer's house to drag on Big Bird while Eli gets blazed out of his mind and tries to spit-swap till the sun comes up. Caution: Go Children Slow.

On the line, Maya's singing with Zoë to some blaring techno tune. "You're up!" she yells. "What's fresh, sweet?"

I laugh. "Not Eli on the other line."

"Whoa! Be easy, betty! Rinse and repeat, right? Hang up with the ex-factor and come get shakes. We got some massive juicy bits to spill."

"What about your date with Man Thong?"

"Ugh," she says. "Dram-o-rama. Come out and we'll scat the whole ugly ordeal. We're talking hotel lobby handies gone bad and Zoë getting thrown in the pool, cracking some flap-Jacks' skulls, and nearly going jailbird. Massive epic, Jack. Massive."

I say I'm in, but before I can hang up with Eli, he makes me promise to dial him back this week, which I probably won't. At the diner, we all get strawberry milkshakes and oyster crackers and, as the night sets and day begins, the Cats plus Gideon word-hemorrhage their night and it's like every which way I turn, sex is in the batter. I just seem to be the only Jack not getting in on the baked goods.

Pretty Pennies

Senior Skip Day. We're at the beach, a clash, rubble-and-trash-strewn excuse for a shore. The seaweed's thick as stew and our class settles into its usual clans and cliques. The bikini-bottomed Stray Cats and I are tossing a Frisbee with some of my track-Jacks and I find a dead stingray by the water's edge. I feel happy and sinister and the gravity of Eve's moon pulls at my watery parts, so I drag the ray up to where the Pretty Pennies are perched on their matching towels by the boardwalk, sunbathing in a row of perfectly roasting flesh, Lycra, hair ties, coconut body oil, and studded cat-eye, movie-star shades. I cross battle lines. I'm an imposter in foreign lands, and I leave my offering of stinking white ray with Ms. Ancient History.

Bowing dramatically, I say, "Your Lordship, Ms. Ancient History," and place a dried seaweed crown on her golden curls. The other Pennies ignore me as they would a green beach fly, the backstabbing, heart-Jack-snatching brunette giving me the death-stare once-over before turning back to the glossy pages of her magazine. But Eve is smiling as she pulls me down by my wrist, hands me chilled cantaloupe and grapes on toothpicks from a cooler.

"Beatstreet," I say, grinning, taking the cold fruit in my mouth.

She laughs. "We simply must stop meeting like this."

I grin and shrug, O-R-S-H-O-U-L-D-W-E, spelling out crisp and neat inside my mind. I tug at the neck of my Bettie Page one-piece, smooth down my bangs. "So, what's on the switch, Eve Brooks? I mean, I've wanted to ask you since forever ago. Ahh . . ." I lower my voice. "How's your eggs?"

"*Eggs?*" she whispers. "What's eggs?"

I scowl, draw two circles in the sand and under them an arc.

"How's my *happyface*?"

"*Eggs*," I hiss. "Like, *ovaries*."

"Oh!" she says, cracking her sunset smile. "The pregnancy test. Yeah. That was hell." She brushes sand from her leg. "It was legit, though. Got my period that night."

"Oh, word?"

"Yeah. But my happyface is good, too."

I smile. I tell her a story. I say, "D'you remember when we were in sixth grade and we went to Roller-Planet and that schemey, pube-'stached Jack camped out at the water fountain and was lunging in to spit-swap the little innocent antelope betties sipping from the watering hole? And you saw it all and heeled it up to the bubbler and, when he pounced on you, you hit him with this massive mouth of chewed-up red hots, leaving the whole mucous-coated fireball in his skeezy oral hole? 'Member?" She nods and I take a breath.

"And then that time we got on the city bus after school to see where it went and it held us hostage for like, three flippin' hours? And the bus driver got off and was all smokin' tars and scratchin' his balls and said, 'I don't give a rat's tail where you live, no way I'm turnin' this goddamn bus around.' And your mom had to cut a wheel practically across the state just to get us?"

She's laughing. "'Of course I do."

I pull a tar from behind my ear and stick it between my lips, but I have no light. I pat my bathing suit like I'm shaking myself down, and shrug, smiling from behind the tar.

She rifles through her large straw bag and finds a loose set of matches.

"Smoking's clash," she says, giving me a light.

"Word," I agree, one eye closed as the smoke wafts up into my mug.

"You should stop."

"Think so?" She nods. I flick the ashes away and then flip the tar around into my mouth. I open my eyes wide and look down with big Ophelia eyes as smoke billows out my nose. My best and most classic party trick.

She's laughing again but says, "Crank, Lu. For real," and I'm blasted with jumbles of words I shift and edit and sort. A poem:

As gulls cry, aloft
Taken by a whispered wind
My name on her lips.

Haiku, courtesy of Lu I-Love-You Butler. I chill easy and dam the words fighting to spill from my mouth as I spin the tar back around and pull it from my lips, studying it. "I'm beatstreet," I say. "I quit," and flick it into the sand.

Eve sighs and picks it up, stubbing it out on a small stone and dropping it into an empty water bottle. "A-plus for dramatic effect, but that doesn't mean you can be some littery little litterbug."

"You always were a better person than me." I take another grape from the plastic plate in her lap.

"Litterbug, litterbug, shame on you," she sings, her out-stretched palms moving back and forth in front of her. "Shame on the terrible things you do. You spoil the soil and the wonderful view. Shame shame shame shame shame on you." She looks up over her sunglasses, beaming, her shoulders skipping with giggles.

I shake my head. "You live in a fantasy land, Ms. Ancient History," and I pour sand grains through my fist. "So I'm a bug, huh? A litterbug?"

"Bugs are massive pesky," she says, pulling off her shades. "So yeah, that's what you are."

I laugh and she's squinting in the sun, her oiled skin glaring and shimmering like the sea's whitest caps. She says something but I'm counting the freckles on her nose.

"*Ground control to Major Lu.* What ever happened with that sweater?"

I shrug, transfixed.

She says, "What're you doing?"

"Research." I say, "Nothing," and pop another cantaloupe into my mouth, fixing her with my best stony-eyed gaze.

"*What?*" She laughs loud, her voice rippling, shimmering in waves over the hot sand, and the Pennies cock their ultra-tweezed brows and glare at us over superfreeze shades. Eve looks at them, laughing, and turns her back to them, her singing giggles like a thrush's liquid call. I'm beside myself. Beyond.

I look into her gray-ocean eyes and she smiles. I quickly look away, but again, my mouth is opening, my brain on total revolt. "'Once she hears to her heart's content, sails on, a wiser Jack.'"

My chest burns. I'm pouring it on like syrup over Sunday-morning pancakes. Eve furrows her brow, her cheeks flushed and rosy, and I shake my head, laughing it off. I look away, mutter, "*The Odyssey*. Reading humor."

"O-*kay*?" she says and reaches out her hand, lays four impossibly long fingers across my wrist. And it's like the whole world is okay. Like everything is all right. And I know I should tell her about Nate. Now would be the perfect time. I take a breath, look up again, and then catch two of the Prickly Pennies eyeing me sidelong. Though it literally slays me, I slide slowly out from under Eve's warm hand.

"Um, I gotta jet," I say, standing, hold up two peace sign digits. "Things to see, people to do. You know."

"Too bad." She frowns and I feel my cheeks go beet-borscht red.

"Rinse and repeat," I smile.

"Later, Beatstreet. Keep it on the real," and I wave, heel it down the beach, back to my Jacks, where Zoë, Maya, and I powwow and decide to go out for pizza. As we're heeling it to Zoë's whip, we pass Amelia Long, sitting on a towel at the end of a row of other misfit betties. She waves

and smiles and I smile and, for some unconscionable reason, invite them all to come with. My apple-jacks give me
the massive stink eye, but I'm actually glad I invited her
and her crew 'cause by the looks of her big mop grin and
blissful seesaw eyebrows, I've just about made her life.

Light, Like Air

Last day of school, *forever*. In the hall, everyone exchanges long, rambling notes written in the backs of yearbooks, and betties hug and cry and hold on for dear life. En Français we have une grande fête. We invite the senior Spanish class to crashpad and Zoë and Maya are there and we scarf on crêpes and fajitas and rock out to Basque and Breton folk music. Zoë pulls a neck muscle headbanging.

I'm slightly sweaty-palmed all day, the goodbye poem

I've written for Ms. Hayes burning in my back pocket, and I pull it out over and over to scrutinize. I will give it to her. I won't. I will. I won't.

I sit in my last class ever with her and we listen to her freshmen give in-n-out group presentations of their theatrical interpretations of *A Separate Peace* and there's an abundance of flip Finnys falling from trees, and many a mop Ophelia Gene, wringing their mitts and cackling Wa ha ha! like Count Dracula.

Ms. Hayes and I laugh and huddle close, making notes on their projects, smiling sweet as peach pie at each student as they speak. Before the bell rings, I say goodbye to the wee-Jacks and get a gaggle of quick, stiff hugs and the betty who's been so crush on me gives me a drawing she did and it breaks my heart in two. As everyone files out, Ms. Hayes gives me a massive Ms. Hayes–scented hug. So close, she feels infinities away.

"You're gonna miss me," I say and she laughs. I know I'll miss her more.

"No kidding," she says. "You better come back to visit once in a while."

"Word," I say. "I will." I look up and she's smiling. "Ugh. I hate goodbyes. I don't know what's wrong with everybody. All this sentimental bullscat. It's like the world is coming to end."

"Never mind about them," she says. "How are you?"

I laugh. "That's a loaded gun."

"Lu," she says. "You're gonna be amazing. I have no doubt whatsoever, *Dr.* Butler. Just promise me you'll squeeze in some lit classes, maybe creative writing, or modern verse. Visual art!"

I nod, knowing I probably won't, what with premed requirements up the wazoo, and she pulls me into another, longer hug. With one final flashing of my pearly whites, I turn to leave, but feel again the poem I scrawled out this morning, just for her, burning bright inside my back pocket. I slide it out and hold it between my digits. It's warm, and feels light, like air. I turn back and she's waiting. I put it in her hand, saying nothing, and heel it on out.

Outside her door, I hyperventilate for a sec and then heel it sort of spaced down the hall, *one, two, three,* counting the forty-one steps from Ms. Hayes's door to my very-soon-to-be locker-no-more. I imagine her reading each word of the poem, reciting it silently in my head:

> *At black hole's edge I turn*
> *Wave at last from the event horizon of her.*
> *Does she see how beautiful she is? Does she know?*
> *I hope.*

Baby Owl

Graduation day. A flock of white-cloaked cogs, we follow each other's backs into the gymnasium and march in line one last time.

I shuffle-step by my family. Dad is dressed massive swank, his stubble shaved, hair gelled. Miles squirms and fidgets in his shirt and tie, pushing the stem of his glasses up his sweaty nose. My sweetbeat little Oma's freshly permed silver curls glow around her head like a halo. And as always, the absence of Mom and my sister-Jack, Marta, looms the ever-present pink elephants. Mom's been on permanent Butler Family Haitus for eons now, so that's no big shocker. And Marta's latest love-'em-and-leave-'em adventure has her seated on a plane to Rome, probably reclining in a plush, cushioned seat, sipping ginger ale as I sweat in my polyester gown. But I can't help but smile and wave as Oma snaps picture after picture on her relic disposable camera as we walk by single file before the seated audience.

Ms. Hayes sits in the second row with other teachers and I wonder how many ceremonies like this she's had to attend. She smiles big as I go by and I swallow deep the uneasy memory of my poem as I commit to my mind the lines around her eyes, the slow curve of her mouth, the contours of her neck. She kills me, she always will.

It's a massive long, sweltering hot ceremony and in response the sky spews its first major late-spring thunderstorm outside the gym's floor-to-ceiling windows. Students, teachers, moms, sisters, dads, uncles, and grannies fan at their dripping mugs and we all trickle and squirm and drip drop dribble in our gowns and skirts and trousers. Eve Brooks is three seats down from mine and I try to catch her eye but she's got this plastered-on, slapped-on, surgically implanted smile on her face. I fold my program into an origami lily, thinking I'll pass it down to her, but next to me, Abby Cortland gushes at it, and I sigh, hand it to her.

"So beat!" she says.

"Rinse and repeat," I whisper, wishing she were Eve.

All in all, it's an utter anticlimax. After the last over-achieving monkey stands down from the podium, nobody throws their caps in the air. In the hall, everyone with their flushed faces and greasy shags are chalky wisps as they mingle in their flash-photographed stupors.

The Butler clan (minus a few) go out for family dinner to a swank restaurant in the city and I wanna invite Zoë to join, liberate her from her degenerate blood relations. But she says she's gotta stick it out, leading a Stone family mission to find some BBQ wings and keno. I wish her Godspeed.

At the table, Oma sits beside me and pats my mitt with her soft, blue-veined, gold-and-diamond-adorned digits. My dad waxes high school sentimental over a plate of crispy calamari tapas and Oma winks and slips me a small wrapped box. I open it and inside's a brandy-new Mickey Mouse wristwatch, white-gloved mitts orbiting in arm-wrenching ellipses around the retro icon's smug little rodent grin. Oma's hazy smile is pleased as cake, as it always is when she sits like the Godfather in her hand-carved rocking chair, doling out mail-order complimentary wrist-watches like hundred-dollar bills. I got two last month.

As I strap Mickey onto my sticky wrist, Miles looks at me with this mischievous grin and we both start cracking up because in an hour it'll be dangling from Spider-Man's boot or the light-up Rudolph and Santa-head pin we all forbade Dad from sporting at Christmastime a thousand years ago.

Miles has this mega-ton of useless junk (armless action figures, broken techno-gadgets, gaudy jewelry, and, of course, many a mail-order wristwatch) that our family's been gifted over the years all hanging on fishing line along the walls of his bedroom. He's massive Ophelia for junk and it's riot as hell. His collection already boasts seven or eight Mickeys, but Miles, the little Trashrat, loves a repeating punch line.

At the table, Oma starts to crack up a bit, spilling her food and forgetting what she's saying mid-sentence. We eat quickly to get back to her house before she conks out comatose in her tortellini. I say I'll take her so Dad can get back to the hospital for work, and I even invite Miles to come with to make him feel like a big kid. Dad looks proud, and a little tired, as Miles and I scoop up our sweetbeat hunched little Oma, who totters between us, her bony arms wrapped in each of ours.

When we drop her off, she makes a big show of walking in circles around her kitchen, trying to pawn off her earthly possessions. Bitsy, her tiny, ankle-terrorizing Chihuahua, yips at us and runs in fits around Oma's mauve orthopedic shoes.

"Oma, stop. I don't *need* anything!" Miles says, his small round mug reddening as she wraps a yellow silk scarf around his thin, sweaty neck. I'm giggling massive as I scheme a tube of her coral lipstick and paint perky geisha lips on my protesting and rather ace little bro. Even Oma's cracking up as she places a dainty, feathered fur hat on his head that slides down and sits on the rim of his glasses.

"*You*," Oma says, "are the spitting image of me fifty-five years ago, Miles Gregory Butler. I was twenty-six years old when I bought that hat and it cost me a week's wages, worth every dime. Your Opa fell in love with me in the hat." Her words warble in a crackly, nostalgic voice, and we are all splitting our sides.

"Yowza," I say, looking through tears at Miles's scowling mug. "You musta been a real looker, Oma," and she hoots, swatting her creaky mitt at me.

As we're shuffling out the door, she slips a stiff, folded twenty into my pocket, money I know she can't spare, and kisses me and Miles one hundred baby-powder-puffing times.

"Remember to thank God every night before bed for all you've been given," she preaches. "I talk to Him all the time. I pray for you. I always pray for you, now. Don't you forget to thank Him. He loves you." From her frail arms, Bitsy yips in punctuation.

"Okay, Oma," Miles says, rolling his eyes at me, wiping pink paint from his lips with the back of his hand.

On the trek home, the rain finally lets up, so we stop for ice cream with Oma's twenty before beating it home. Still superfreeze in our wrinkly formal gear, we lean against the hood of my banger, shooting the breeze. I slide Mickey from my wrist.

"Here ya go, Trashrat," I say, and he grins, shoving it in his pocket.

He leans back, takes a pensive lick of ice cream. "D'you remember Opa, Lu?"

I nod. "Word. He was pretty loopy, though. 'Cause of the war. But cool, too. Massive cool."

Miles looks up at the clearing sky. "I wish I could have known him better. But I was so young when he died."

I laugh. "Miles, he died two years ago."

"I know," he says solemnly. "I didn't understand things like I do now."

I almost laugh again, at how massive serious he's being, but I don't and appreciate for a half second that even for a genius he's kind of adorable. I slurp up my black raspberry with chocolate sprinkles until I get to the cone, and then give him the rest (his favorite part). Then my speak rings and Zoë and Maya are wondering where the flip I've been their whole lives.

I herd Miles back into my banger and he stares out the window as I call Castle and Rabbit and we round up a gaggle of Jacks for a post-graduation toaster. We decide a pool is a must-have, so everybody's looking to crashpad my house and I call Dad and he says the more the merrier, just don't invite Al Coholic. Yuk yuk. I say of course, and not fifteen minutes after Miles and I pull in, the lantern-lit pool is spilling over its edges with kids crammed into every cranny and nook. It's a strange brew of my track-Jacks, the city crew, and Maya's ever-revolving male entourage. But an odd harmony's found and I relax into the mismatched randomness of the night.

Dad, back from saving lives, shuffles around awkwardly for a bit, achieving new heights of mortification with every gesture, making small talk with Zoë and Maya, grilling about college and the summer to come. Miles gets massive zoomies and tears around in his swim shorts, near hysterical with excitement, cannonballing shrieking betties in the deep end and chugging down heaping mittfuls of chips and cookies. He's teetering on sugar-induced seizure status after mainlining two cans of orange pop, when Dad mercifully launches into the "Time for pj's, brush teeth, and tinks" bedtime routine.

"Da-ad!" Miles balks, but, thank-ye-jesus, traipses heavily up to bed.

With Dad MIA, Jacks crack secretly stashed brews and the stereo is turned up loud. A few hours in, I catch sight of Miles curled like a baby owl in a dark window, peering down at all the glossy full-grown shavers and betties. We play music and dance and laugh. There's a drunk diving contest (not safe) and then a massive water-noodle war (epic) that morphs into semi-nude noodle tag in the yard. And all the while my wee brother-Jack sits with his small fingertips perched on the windowsill and I know he wishes he were big, too. I know, too, someday he'll learn not every night is as switch and easy as this one seems to be.

Thumb War

ext morning my apple-Jacks and I peel ourselves off my TV room couch and stroll into the diner and who else but the flesh-and-bones Ms. Ancient History is sitting with the Pretty Pennies in a shiny orange-and-blue plastic booth. We pass their table and smile hellos and Eve holds my gaze a little bit long. Our crowds are universes apart. They are queens of the hive. We are ants. They are honey. We are not impressed. But we are.

The Cats sit in the booth behind theirs and scat and laugh too loud. After ice cream sundaes shaped like clown faces, I can't help myself—I turn around and pull Ms. Ancient History's curlicue hair. She swivels and I look away and scheme it wasn't me. She whistles, poorly, as she drops an ice cube down the back of my shirt and I yelp and grab for it as it runs down my back and into my skinnies. She's cracking up and me, I'm a soaking mess.

"It's on," I challenge. "One, two, three, four, I declare a thumb war."

"Five, six, seven, eight, try to keep your thumb straight." She grabs hold of my hand.

"Nine, ten, let's begin."

I win, but only after we establish there's no "snake in the grass" or "tag team" schemer tactics allowed. Eve's got an advantage, as her thumbs are oddly flexible and I suspect, double-jointed. But I talk massive trash and she laughs. BAM! She's pinned. I win. She is Sore Thumb Loser.

"You're all thumbs, Brooks," I laugh.

She tells me about a toaster going hit tonight. "In the woods," she says. "Under Suicide Bridge, by the lake, nine p.m. You Jacks should be in." And we shake on it and agree to a rematch. The Pretty Pennies stand and throw their tip of crumpled dollars on the table and we watch as they sway and shimmy out the large swinging door.

I turn back to the Cats and see in their expressions that I'm a traitor, a treasonous double agent. They give me massive stink eye, but I also know Zoë and Maya are squirming with excitement.

"Word, so we scrounge up some sleeping bags and brew." Zoë grins and we are heads down in super-stealth planning mode.

"Yo, Drug-Free," I poke at Maya. "Got any ideas?" And we're all cracking up, balance restored. As we talk, I picture my retro Ninja Turtles sleeping bag and know Eve will be hit for it. I can't wait.

While loitering at Maya's criminal cousin's ramshackle trailer, hoping to score some tars and sauce, I get a buzz from Dad saying *Oma's okay.* Which is weird 'cause I didn't know she maybe wasn't. I dial Miles, then Dad, to no avail. Finally I get Auntie Kay on the line and she says things like *unexplained bleeding, needles, transfusions.* I get a little woozy, my neck prickling and chilled. She says they're hiring a nurse to camp at Oma's place overnight, maybe for the rest of the week. Just in case. But, really, she's *fine.*

"Sounds serious," Zoë says, shaking her head at Maya, who's shamelessly flirting up her hillbilly blood relation in the glare of the Chariot's headlights. "All that *blood.*"

I shiver. "Y'think? But my aunt says she's okay."

Zoë shrugs. "You're the one wants to be a doctor."

"A surgeon, dummy."

"What, surgeons don't see *blood*?"

I shiver again.

"Blood." Zoë grins and I punch her in the arm. She laughs, rubbing at where I socked her. But then she says, "Y'know, we don't have to toast tonight, if you're not feeling it. I'd get that."

"Naw," I say after a bit. "Oma's a hard nut. I'll go scope her tomorrow. Plus, Kay said she's gonna be fine. Right now I just wanna get sauced with my apple-Jacks."

"Word, Jack."

Booze Pirates

We're standing around a bonfire: the Stray Cats, the Hit-Jacks, the Stranger-Jacks, the Massive Flap-Jacks, the Pretty Pennies, and their Gaggle of Doting Minions.

Maya's massive flip, acting the odd man out. Zoë and I manage to keep our wits about us and are having a grand ole time. We socialize, we mingle. We're super switch. We're also far, far more sauced.

Maya shivers and whines. "Let's jetset," she says. And, "I'm freezing."

I say, "All right, clash-Jacks, who stole my left shoe?"

Zoë and I pilfer brews from large, manly coolers. And I find her, Ms. Ancient History Sore Thumb Loser, and amble over, walking a crooked line. I gift her one of my schemed brews and Nate Gray's by her side, giving me a warm-as-peach-pie smile. I smile, too, but only with my eyes.

He says, "Lucy Butler, that's so switch of you to gift Eve your brew." I shrug and with a shifty grin hide my other full brew in my zip-up hoodie pouch.

"Look, Mom, no tars," I announce to Eve, holding up my empty mitts.

"Beatstreet." She grins but then Nate is leaping aloft to snag an errant football lobbed over the fire, hard-bumping into Eve, who shrieks, her brew slipping from her hand and into the dirt. She moans, head back, and I lean over to scoop it up and then she's close, by my side, her warm, boozy breath in my ear. "Gotta pee," she says, so we heel it to the edge of the clearing, her warm hand yanking mine.

I crack open my brew and chug as I pee.

"Pesky Bug, can't you wait until you're done?" she scolds, steadying her sauced self on a tree trunk.

"It's so flip," I say. "It's, like, in one end, out the other."

"Crank!" she hoots as she's zipping her fly, tipping

over laughing like it's the riotest thing she's ever heard. I catch her, but fall, too—two loose screws and she's grabbing my wrist and doesn't let go and we're ass-down in the twigs and leaves. Then there's a snap-crack in the woods and we freeze, holding our breaths. We wait. "BTs!" she hisses.

"What?"

"BTs! Bathroom Trolls! We're the BTs of Suicide Bridge!" she yells and we're cracking up massive and I can smell her hair and it's like oranges and ginger and clove. We're still hysterical as we return to the fire too soon and I linger, swaying, as she resumes her position at Nate's side and he pulls her in, wrapping ape-long arms around her from behind and she is His Betty. Nate's Girl. If it's possible, I'm liking him less.

Zoë comes by, tugging me by my sleeve, and I hold up peace sign digits and Eve laughs, rosy cheeks all aglow. "I know, I know," she says. "Rinse and then do it again," and I give her a wink and a nod and heel it away. Zo and I slink off in search of more coolers and are booze pirates once more, Yo ho!

Eve never does see my Ninja Turtles sleeping bag. She heels it in a dark moment through the trees and shrubs with Nate I'd-Never-Cheat-on-You-Baby Gray and Zoë and I squeeze into my sleeping bag in a tent with six other flap-Jacks and our group is like sardines in a can, stench included. Maya's long gone many hours past. We're not sure how or with whom.

Night is short, and in the morning as we break down the tent Eve's flap-Jacks are all, "Next weekend. Same time, different place. Clay Beach, Green Lake," and the Pennies draw a rough map with a crayon from the floor of their massive swank whip, bumpy red lines indicating a turn here, a tree there, a large circle for the lake and a smaller one for the brewkeg. The brunette pours it on thick as molasses seeing as I didn't spill beans on her and Nate. Zoë and I smile and fool with them a bit before heeling it to suck down pancakes and bacon at the diner to jive stories of the sauced things we did the night before.

"They're not such clash cogs after all," Zoë says as she pulls into my drive. "They're actually sorta hit."

"I'm not quite final sale on that," I say. "But they're kill to toast with."

"Word," she says, looking at me. "So what's the beat with Eve Brooks? Are you Jacks hit again?"

I shrug. "I suppose we sort of are."

"Word. I was just wondering. Not that you need my permission, obviously. I just thought it seemed massive random. She certainly seemed happy to see your ugly mug last night."

I laugh. "I guess I just like giving her a hard time. She's beat, y'know? Different from the rest."

"Well, I'm not quite final sale on that. But I'll take your word on it."

She cuts the engine and sighs and I think maybe she's a wee bit steamed. I fidget in my seat, watch a wild cotton-tailed bunny dash across the neighbor's front lawn next door.

"Y'know," she lays in. "Nate Gray is massive cheating on her. Maya heard it a while back and then last night there were some flap-Jacks scatting it up. You should probably spill it to her. Now that you're bestest apple-Jacks again."

I let her snark slide, not wanting to get into it. Or worse, give myself away.

"Maybe."

I open the door and Zoë's rubbing her sleepy-eyed mug, giving me the once-over. "She's getting massive skinny, too, don't you think? I thought maybe she was yak-king up her food but everyone says she just doesn't eat." I just nod, snagging my sleeping bag from the back and slid-ing out.

Halfway up the back stairs I remember to wave good-bye, but when I turn, Zoë's whip is already gone.

I drag my bones up to the back porch and I see through the glass that Dad is hunched over a bagel and a cuppa joe at the kitchen island and there's nowhere to go but in.

"Guten Morgen, mein Vater," I say, pulling on a half grin and plopping my Ninja Turtles bag down onto the counter.

He scans me like an X-ray. "Lookin' a little rough there, camper."

I shrug. "What can I say, it was *in-tents*."

"That's my joke." He smiles. I snag half a bagel off his plate and jam it in my mouth. "So, your Oma," he says.

"I know. I talked to Auntie Kay. I was thinking I could heel it on over there later, bring her some ice-cold double chocolate crunch." Though the thought of doing so makes me a bit queasy.

He nods. "We'll see. She needs to rest right now. We all just need to rest."

"Word," I say and look at my dad, notice how disheveled he is—his threads wrinkled, tie on crooked, a small red stain on the cuff of his shirtsleeve. I shiver, wonder whose it is. "Lots of parties these days, kiddo," he sighs. "Miles said he found some beer cans in the woods."

"Little Trashrat," I groan. "Those are for sure his, Dad. Don't let him fool you."

Dad rolls his eyes. "Just . . ." He trails off as a buzz on his speak comes in.

"Just?" I say.

"Just can it."

"Haha. *Can* it?" But Dad is clicking away, lost to the void. I see my window and make a stealthy escape, relieved I'm not busted, and head upstairs, my soft cushy cloud bed beckoning. I heel it by Miles's door and chuck my sleeping bag at his head and feel a wee twinge of regret when he wakes with a frightened squeal.

"Narc," I say half-heartedly and schlep off down the hall to sleep for the next two billion years.

On the Verge

I'm completely caught in the middle. Slow and coma all day, I'm on the verge of total mind melt, lying like a useless sack of meat in my bed. Eli buzzes and says he misses me and we should get into it again. I lie in bed and think about buzzing him back, telling him I'll heel it on over and we can drag tars and swap spit in his dingy den and maybe together find some of that powdered white slip. It would be so easy. Too easy. I could even have sex with him again, I guess. It's basically all I can think about, sex. But not with Eli.

Eve is no longer Ancient History.

I let thoughts of her creep and spread through me, my new Never-Ending Pending, my mind on her like flame on spilt gasoline. I think about her hand around my wrist. And her perfume. And her lips. I think about her crank heart-Jack. And her hand. And her lips.

I think about what the soft warmth of her skin would feel like pressed against mine, sliding against me, pushing, in my mouth. How she would taste. I think about her fingers on my back, gripping me, pulling. And her hand. And her lips.

I worry about Oma. And then switch back to brooding over Eve. I half consider dishing everything to Maya, feeling I might burst if I keep it all inside. I think maybe she'd listen and keep the Eve stuff on the DL and I even buzz her *What's fresh, Drug-Free?* but she doesn't buzz back. I know that even if she did I'd prolly lose my nerve. I don't even think of dialing Zo.

I call Oma's and the speak just rings and rings.

So, I just sit at home and pine and suffer alone.

I get up and run miles upon miles, and pine and suffer alone.

I shower, and pine and suffer alone.

I lie here in bed, and pine and suffer alone.

And I love it.

No Big Whoop

I'm in my weekend tank top and boxers, finally getting around to loading gas into the lawn mover, accepting my fate of riding around in circles on the bouncing, stinking seat of the ride-on mini tractor, when I glance at my speak and see Dad has dialed three times and even left a voice mail, which sets off alarm bells. I jog back into the quiet cool dampness of the garage and press play.

"Lucy, your aunts are here at the hospital. Oma's not doing well, we admitted her again and they're running more tests.

But it doesn't look good. I don't know, honey, this is pretty seri-ous. Call me."

I stand there, frozen from top to toe, counting the sec-onds in my head to let my brain reset. I replay his message, thinking if I hear it again I'll understand what this could actually mean. It's not feeling real, not even a little.

I dial back and get him first ring, which makes me even more tweaked.

"Honey, I'm so sorry," his shell-shocked voice says, the beep and blip of hospital noises and my brother's high-pitched voice calling for him in the background. "She says she's done, Lu. No more transfusions. Do you understand? It means she's only got a little time left. A week or two, at most. She wants to be in her own house with all of us, and your aunts and I are gonna help her with that. She's tired, Lu. She's ready to go."

"No," I say. "I thought she was fine. Everybody said she was fine." I swallow down a lump the size of my fist and feel my speak getting hot against my ear.

"I'm so sorry, Lucy," he says again, but then Miles is cry-ing and I'm handed off to my aunt who, with military preci-sion, tells me I can either pick up my god-awful sister at the airport or go to Oma's house and take apart her bed to make space for the medical equipment hospice care is providing. I opt for the latter and she says they'll be there soon, so I better hustle and I almost ask her what hospice means exactly, but then I don't. She says this is Oma's choice and it's not easy and everyone's dealing with it in their own way. She says my Oma's brave. Very brave.

I just say, "Okay."

In the glass of the creaky front door, I catch a glimpse of my sad-sack face. I wanted to cry the whole way over but couldn't. I think maybe I've forgotten how.

In the kitchen, Bitsy greets me with yips and snarls from under the old wooden dining set and I flick on the overhead light and stare at Oma's place mat on the table, empty bowl, clean spoon on top, a tub of chocolate ice cream I discover is soup when I pull open the lid.

I find an old flat-head screwdriver and sweat and grunt while I break down her and Opa's old bed and then vacuum at least three decades' worth of animal and human hair from the musty, pink-hued carpet. My two younger shaver-Jack twin cousins, useless as ever, pull up in my aunt's van, and half-heartedly help me haul Oma's mildewed bedspring down her perilously steep cellar stairs. At the bottom I nearly send Bitsy's skull careening into drywall as she whips past my feet to ransack her stored feed below. I chase her around the cellar for a few dusty minutes and then sneeze my way back up into the living room, where the boys turn on SportsCenter and glue their eyeballs to the screen.

Then Jesse From Hospice is knocking at the front door, rushing in with clipboard and badge, rambling at breakneck pace as I try and work the gears of my brain back to life. I remind myself I'm premed and can handle high-intensity medical banter as he's loading in an oxygen machine and tank and a heart monitor and this almost-toilet thingy on wheels I should know the name of, but somehow, right now, can't seem to remember.

Then comes Oma's replacement bed, a glorified hospital cot on glistening steel limbs and I'm getting panicky as I help Jesse From Hospice pop this lever into that hole, this hinge into that socket, until it stands freely. And then he's rattling on, telling me how to start up the Beep-Beep machine and how to hook Oma in and how the oxygen tank might explode if you push this button here, but on the other hand it probably wouldn't even if you did, but just in case, *don't*.

And I'm a slow-crumbling mass of brick and mortar, loose bits shedding and skipping in my clumsy, fragmented wake. I'm covered in cool, clammy sweat, a death grip of cold fear wrapping icy-hot fingers around my neck. I'm blinking my eyes, trying to focus on his lips moving and a faint buzzing sounds in my ears, a transparent green sheath of fuzz descends on my sight in a vibrating wave. And just then Dad and my aunts come ripping into the house and Jesse From Hospice gives them the same exact spiel and

Dad's a doctor, so everything's under control, he's seen this all before. No big whoop. None at all.

I prop myself in a stiff, high-backed formal chair in the corner of Oma's room and breathe. Breathe. Breathe. And I'm doing okay, getting my head clear as order is restored with armloads of sheets and a quilt and a pillow on the thing looking more and more like an actual bed, when lo and behold here comes my Oma.

They're rolling her up Opa's old wheelchair ramp and they push her through the door and instantly stale body-and-rubbing-alcohol-scented musty wafts color the suddenly overcrowded bedroom. Oma's sedated head lolls, with tubes in her nose, an IV in her rice-paper wrist, bruises up her arm, and the palest of pale, blue-tinted skin. I feel a dark, hot weight on my back and legs and arms, crawling, creeping, clinging. And more cars are pulling into the drive and the ambulance is backing out and here she is and this is all really happening.

And me, I can't do it. I just can't deal.

And I'm gone—to the clattering voices of the aunts bickering, the dark, moody pools of Bitsy's bugged-out eyes, Oma's unkempt snow-white curls, her tiny feet like skeleton bones inside Bigfoot's woolen socks, tubes pumping this and that out of her thin, frail body, blood, skin.

I'm gone, heeling it outside into the cheery late-morning sun, too cheery. I leap into my banger to find I'm boxed in by all the new arrivals, so I wheel quick around the far side of her house, bumping over flowerbeds to make my hasty, sweaty-mitted escape.

Marta is climbing from Dad's truck and she catches my eyes, hers rimmed in sooty black from freshly shed tears.

Thank you, call again.

Whirling Dervish

I finally navigate home from my tree in the graveyard, after many an hour trying—unsuccessfully—to shake the feeling that scrappy-Jacks in coveralls are running a car wash between my ears. Assuming things couldn't get any worse, I pull into my street to find my sister and her old gang of high school flap-Jacks have hijacked 211 Maple Way, and am reminded that when Mart's in the mix, there are always new heights of terrible one is able to experience.

I park behind a line of crooked bangers way up the road

and walk and stare out at the multitude of retro-Jacks milling about, scatting, and dragging canna on the lawn, their tripped-out psychedelia tunes blasting and echoing into the still cul-de-sac of our sterile neighborhood. I wasn't aware a family member's imminent demise was reason to throw down a massive-blaster toaster and I'm planning to tell my sister this when Mistress Medusa herself saunters up.

"Word, sis," she says, voice low and cold. "By the way, thanks for the sunshiney welcome home." All her Jacks dress like it's 1969 and my sister is no exception, with tight leather pants, a batik-patterned shirt, knee-high suede moccasins, and twists of purple and gold embroidery floss tied in her long black hair.

"Totally, man. Far out," I say, stepping back and crossing my arms, waiting for the crazy to be unleashed.

"Oh, yeah, and way to cheese out right when Dad and Miles needed you most. Classy move."

"Yup." I nod, and I try to slip by her but she snags my arm hard, spinning me around.

"*Lucy,*" she says, her freakishly strong mitt crushing my bones.

"Back off," I hiss.

"Why should I?"

"Because I said so. Because I can't deal with *you* right now." I rub my eyes. "I'm on overload, Mart."

"That's not an excuse."

"Actually, Dr. Phil, I didn't ask your opinion."

"Okay, okay," she says, stepping back. "All I'm saying is that just because you're an emotional infant doesn't mean you can act a flap-Jack and skip out on the hard stuff. This isn't about you."

"Oh, that's rich. Miss Missing in Action. Thanks for the life advice."

She yanks a huge pair of shades over her Ice Queen eyes. "Listen, *whatever.* I don't need your flap-scat right now. And I don't care if you wanna toast with us, Lu, just don't go dime-dropping Dad."

"Seriously, Mart, what is your damage? I'm not, like, seven years old. I'm not Miles. I'm no rat."

"Well, nobody needs to know. They're all gonna conk out at Oma's, where she's laid up, prepping herself to *die*, surrounded by her wonderful and loving family. But you wouldn't know anything about that." And that's the last straw: I slam into her, my shoulder smashing into hers, her body careening back into the railing. She yelps, glaring at me, mouth wide, as I finally push by to snag the handle of the back porch door. Some short, shaggy skuzzer with pale skin and massive long dreads strides up to her side to comfort her, sliding a mitt down her snooty, heart-shaped heinie. She turns from me in a rage.

"Clash-JACK," I hiss after her as they heel it away into the woods.

"EMOTIONAL INFANT!" she yells for the whole goddamn

world to hear and I roll my eyes, spit a big, crank loogie on the grass. Oh, sugary sisterly love.

And then this massive dreamy shaver, Blue, is sauntering up and he's smiling, cracking up at what a clash cog my sister is being. "What a drag," he chuckles, slipping a lit tar between my lips. And then he's lolling away.

I wander alone, after washing away my rage in a searing hot shower, heeling it coma through my house sipping a stolen brew. And then another. Another still. My body becomes light, aloft, and I chain-drag tars. It's bright and strange and when I'm alone in the bathroom my mug in the mirror is eons away. I park by an open box of pizza in the kitchen and see Marta heeling it up the stairs, some thick-paged book tucked under her leather-fringed arm.

"The flip?" I drunkenly call out to the sharp line of her shadowed back.

"I'm going to bed," she sighs and continues to climb. I pound after her.

"All your sauced-Jacks are still here, lying out all over the goddamn lawn. You can't just go to bed."

"Whatever. It's late. I'm hacked. They'll get the point."

"Unreal," I say, blink my blurry eyes. "You're really something, Jack. One of a flipping kind. A real role model."

"Y'know, Lu," she hisses, "Oma's *dying*. Have you even said two words to her? There isn't much time."

"What, did you pop an Oxy tonight in her name tonight, Gandhi? Snuff some snow just for her?" and she snorts, stomps away. I turn, stride back down the hall. The screen door opens and tunes blare in from outside. I shuffle over to the sink, gulp down glass after glass of water, my temples pounding, my brains sloshing about, half wondering why I don't cruise my sad sack on upstairs, too.

Instead, I sit on the lawn and drag too much canna from Marta's Jacks' tight, hand-rolled joints. And then I'm pedal-to-the-metal floored when none other than Dream Queen Gazelle Raine Hall, the Crush That Broke the Camel's Back, is strutting across the grass, kill blond tresses taking flight, and when she walks she floats and her legs are so long you could heel it underneath and she would have no idea. Somehow the fates align and she magically materializes by my side.

"Wee-Butler? Is that you, all growd up?"

"Raine Hall!" I grin, my eyes two slitty slits. "You're at my house! So Ophelia."

She tilts back her head and laughs out loud, tells me to come with for a toke in the woods and I'm so deep-fried I actually follow her into the trees and she pulls me, snaking, through the crowded baby pines.

I open my mouth but Raine's swinging an arm around my shoulder, a canna pipe finding its way between her lips. "Man-o, Butler. I remember when you were just a wee li'l sprout." I lean in to give her a light and she inhales. She smells like dirt, earth, patchouli. It's amazing. "You're getting massive ace, you know that?" and my head sputters and spits, sparks flying between my ears.

"Me?"

She laughs. "Like Marta. Shavers were so hit for that betty. Probably still are. They must go *Ophelia* for you," and she's eyeing me, blowing a long stream of white smoke from the corner of her mouth. She leans in close, studying my face, and I'm near coma I'm so flip. "You know we swapped spit, one time. Me and your sis?"

"Um." I gulp, try not to picture it. But of course I do. It bothers me how much I like it.

She brushes her hair from her face and I squirm, shift on my feet. "I remember you drawing pictures of me in French," she says. "Telling me all of your worldly woes. Remember that?"

Let me try again, I think, but nod, instead. "Maybe."

She raises the pipe to my mouth and I'm pretty sure it's a terrible idea.

"Y'know, I can't wait to get the flip outta this crank town." She shakes her pretty head. "It's such a hole. I wanna take off, jetset, drop outta State School. Maybe sail rich people's boats from here to the Caribbean. What do you think?"

"You should for sure do that. You'd be like Blackbeard, or Captain Kidd. Like, Ahoy, me hearties! And thar she blows!" and I hate myself for being so crispy as she flashes me a goofy grin and leans down to finish my hit. Our faces are inches apart, and just as I open my mouth to say the most brilliant thing I've ever said, a gaggle of flap-Jacks saunter into the clearing.

"Word, peeps!" Raine whoops, grinning, snagging my light and skipping away. She glances back at me once, cocks an eyebrow, and turns away and it's as if I no longer exist. *POOF*, I'm gone. I stand there for a minute, my head a soggy, foggy day, and seeing as I no longer exist, I push my sorry-sack back through the trees and navigate the labyrinth that is my backyard.

In the living room, I sink deep into the cushions of the big red couch and I feel tiny, invisible, and my digits and feet are almost too miniature to see. I don't know why but in my haze of gloom, Mr. Blue Sky comes by, crash-padding heavy by my side, and he looks at me, through me, smiling, the spiky stubble on his upper lip rippling like a sea of tiny needles. I approximate a grin, or what I remember one was when I still had lips and teeth, and then his long, bony digits take my mitt and he's reading my palm. He tells me I have a solid heart line and an even bolder clothesline. And I can't help myself, I'm cracking up as he takes the laces from my low-tops and we sit and play cat's cradle for millennia.

"So," Blue says, leaning back after our five hundredth game, fixing me in his cerulean gaze. "What's your deal, Mini-Mart? I mean, what's the beat? Such an infinite aura. And yet, so melancholy. Why?"

"Um," I mumble. "Dunno. Maybe it's 'cause my tiny little Oma's gonna up and die and she's, like, the most perfect human I've ever known. Maybe that has something to do with it."

"Word," he says. "I heard about your elder's voluntary exit, Jack. Marta told. She's pretty torn up." I scoff as he sits forward and pushes a stray strand of hair from my face. "But I think it's something else, Jack. Something deeper. Existential-style."

I shrug him off but he's fixed me in his dreamy-Blue-laser-beam stare and so I think, think, think. The blurry shape of an answer vibrates, blowing like soft snow in my mind. "I suppose, well, it's my heart, see?"

Blue nods. "Most assuredly."

"Always been broke," I say. "No, I mean. Yeah. And there's no end in sight. Just sand, dunes, more sand. Not even a desert mirage. Not a drop to drink." I stop, frown. Half forget what the question was.

"Ah." He smiles, studying my face. "Sounds poetic, Jack."

"I assure you it's not."

He stands, stretching up his long arms, fingers grazing the smooth grain of the impossibly lofty ceiling. He looks down from his towering height, slips me back my laces. "Whatever it is, Jack. You gotta own it. Or it'll own you."

"Eh," I grunt. "Life is pain. Didn't you get the memo?"

"We'll see," and he leans over to kiss me softly on the cheek before turning and loping out of view.

"Will we?" I mutter, and for a lifetime I slump coma, on the couch, singing over and over to myself a little ditty: "Se-cret. Re-gret. For-get. You bet. Ciga-rette," on an endless repeat. It's a chart topper, for sure. Then I get all slo-mo OCD and spell each word out, fitting spaces and hyphens into random places, feeling the different sizes and rhythms on my tongue. Just me and my obsessive anxiety disorder, having a blast, when the retro hits streaming through the stereo go mute and then this kill tune Zoë and I are mas-sive crazed for comes blaring on. And it's too good to be true. I'm bopping my head, the beats streaming through my veins like heavy, liquid bliss, and Blue, he's standing above me, arms out, grin wide with happy mischief in his eyes and he's grabbing my mitts and pulling me through the tangle of half-coma hippie-Jacks laid out all over the floor.

"Saw your name on this mix, Jack," he hollers. "Thought you could use a little auditory healing." And right there he starts slicing it up. His big feet go quick-stepping, limbs flail-ing, whole body careening in mad joy to the crunchy beats and I'm laughing so hard at his crazy octopus arms I can barely breathe.

"You really mean what you said," I yell, leaning into him. "About, like, poetry, and owning it, or whatever?"

He grins. "Broken heart, that's not such a bad rap. Just means y'got something real, something worth the good fight. Most don't even have that. Most are dead already."

And I stop, my laughter fading away. I let his words sink slowly in.

And I think of Oma.

Not living, but dying. Actively. Confronting the void.

Eyes wide open.

And I think of Eve Brooks, and Ms. Goddamn Hayes, and me. Lucy Butler. Lost out at sea. Shipwrecked, but swimming to shore. Alive and well.

And I look at Blue, dancing, a whirling dervish.

And I stare out at the heaps of lost, frozen souls passed out coma on the floor, and see in the hard lines of their faces, their waxing, hot misery reaching out, seeking my own, pulling like ugly green ghouls at the cords of thickening, growing sadness coiled about my going-bitter bones. And I shudder. I shiver. I slap a clammy mitt to my face, shake my head side to side. Hard, and harder still.

"Wake up!" I yell, startling myself, and Blue tips back his head and howls at the moon in the skylighted ceiling.

"Wake it up, Jack! Ah-ouuuuuuu!" he screams and I'm gritting my teeth, the music rattling my clenched, ham-bone jaw, my skin prickling with heat as I yank my hood over my head and look down, see my feet already shifting and lifting to the beats, and my body, it's moving in electro-spectro club-kill waves, locks, and pops. And through my red-rimmed, half-lidded vision, my house, it turns circus-tent-striped, fat with skunky-smoked mirth, fog.

Possibility.

I close my eyes, wonder, with a flicker of light blazing bright through my brain, if maybe Blue's words are true. Maybe he's right. *Own it, Jack*, he says. *Own it.* And I think of Eve, I think of No Longer Miss Ancient History and the Pretty Pennies' party tomorrow night at Clay Beach, Green Lake.

And then the song is clanging to its crunchy, perfect end and next thing I know I'm blowing Blue a kiss, ducking under his octopus arms, and heeling it on outta my house, loading headfirst onto my ten-speed spin, making deep tracks over the lawn with the thin strips of my tires. I burn up my hill in record time and the sweet night air is like a calming balm to my saddle-sore soul and I let the rush of Blue's words and the speed of my bike fill my veins with hope and joy. The night is quiet to its core and I'm louder inside then I can ever remember being.

And I'm cruising the seven miles across town to Oma's. I don't know why, it's just what I do.

It's exactly where I want to be.

Into the Sea

Oma, she's deep asleep, head back, heavy against her pillow, cloud-white hair a fuzzy halo about her thin pink skull. Her heavy breathing moves her lips in and out, in and out. The gadgets hooked into her arm and under her shirt go Beep Beep and her chest rises slowly. But it rises, and that's something.

Bitsy's curled up, eyes closed, pressed into Oma's thigh, and I see Dad slouched in the corner in Opa's old recliner, head back, snoring. Miles is passed out coma in his lap.

"Bits," I whisper. "C'mon, Bits," I say, patting at my leg and her lids crack open. "Wanna go for a walk? Wanna be a good girl? Gotta scat?" Her nose twitches and her tail shifts, wags once. But her eyes, they slip closed again.

And everything is still.

I take a deep breath of the musky, body-scented air. But my skin, instead of crawling and itching, begging me to flee, it shimmers still with the night. Awake. Alive, with Blue's gangly arms waving in the dank air of my den, and my body moving like liquid fire to the beats, my heart, broken always, shattered, but thumping and pumping inside. I can still feel the vast night sky shimmering above as I pedaled below, just me, coasting one black tar meter at a time, summer's breeze enveloping my vibrating skin in its humid embrace.

Bitsy adjusts her miniature nose under my Oma's hand and lets out a tiny sigh.

"Word," I say. "I hear that," and take a long look at my stoically wilting old gram. I take the sight of her in, and the smell, and the sound. I wonder what she's dreaming, as she inches ever closer. My sweet little Oma. Dad, sleeping still in the corner, shifts and lets out a fart. *Ducks*, he would say, and I stifle a laugh as I shuffle off onto the musty, empty screened porch around the far side of Oma's house, to end the longest day ever on the world's least comfortable wicker sofa.

I can't sleep at first, but that's okay as I listen to the peepers outside in the pond, the Beep Beep of Oma's heart, and the Slam Slam of my own in my chest and wonder again if Blue's words could possibly be true.

We'll see, I think. *We'll see.*

<hr>

A few hours later, I wake, my mind massive blur and spinning, my body alive and electric. I can't remember where I am until I hear the faint clatter of the five thousand clocks in Oma's living room strike four. I get up to pee and then try to find sleep again on my porch perch, but the sauce still pulsing through my blood drums between my legs and I shift and squirm, toss and turn.

Impressions of Raine Hall cascade in a torrent through my mind, a soaking wet deluge, and my brain aches for sleep but my switch is on, a current passing beneath my skin. I'm lost deep in fantasy as I open my mouth and Raine's invisible lips meet mine. I rise and fall with the movement of my fingers between my legs, but her face is flickering and fading quick. But the drum between my legs is persistent percussion and Raine's features morph and fade into a bright, glowing fog and out of this sunny, backlit haze emerges the image of Ms. Ancient History, Eve Brooks, her freckled face squinting into my eyes, a smile curling the edges of her full strawberry lips. She's laughing and her long cattail fingers are a search-and-rescue mission as they seek and find.

She's like warm water on my arctic skin as her body

presses gently into mine, her soft voice sweet sugar in my ears. *Beatbug*, she whispers as I rise and fall, slowly, and I'm easy and calm as I'm lulled over the edge by my quiet lust. My breath comes deep, my heart cage pounds, my body aches for more, but I lie still. Heavy and clear. I curl onto my side and hug a dog-scented pillow to my chest. I imagine my arms wrapping around Eve's warm body and hot, raw tears come in fiery drops from my closed-shut eyes as I rock my imaginary lover to sleep.

I dream Oma and I are walking, hand in hand, into the sea.

Shrapnel

Over morning OJ, granola, and a hangover the metric weight of King Kong, Dad comes into Oma's kitchen and gives me the parental once-over. I can only imagine what a washed-up sad sack I look like this morning, what with my frizzed-out braids, bloodshot eyes, brains smoking from the holes of my ears.

He sits down beside me and his steady, measured presence pulls at my scratchy lids, my limbs crying out to curl up against him and sleep for a hundred thousand years.

Even so, I still can't shake last night's lingering jazz of possibility.

"Well, Daughter," he says, pouring us each a steaming cuppa joe. "Didn't know you were joining the sleepover party. We could have painted each other's toenails and talked about makeup."

I chuckle, shovel in a spoonful of crunchy goodness. Miles walks in, plunks down on a stool, and picks up a bowl and spoon.

"Y'know, Louie," Dad says, rubbing his face. "I don't *think* it would kill you to call, like *ever*. Tell me where you're at, what's going on, everything's okay."

"Yeah, Louie," Miles says, spitting milk. "It wouldn't kill you to call."

Dad takes a breath. "Luce, you smell . . . And look at you . . . ," he groans. "I get that it's graduation and all, but c'mon, kid, pull yourself together. We got ourselves a family crisis on hand."

My brother nods. "A family crisis."

"Miles, can it," Dad says, and Miles looks at me, giggles.

I look hard at Dad's creased-around-the-edges eyes, study the small scar at the crux of his chin. He watches me warily me from behind the heavy bags under his bloodshot eyes.

"What?"

"Where'd you get that?" I say, pointing my dripping

spoon at his chin. "I never noticed it before." Miles leans in, too, takes a good look.

Dad furrows his brow, sits forward. "Louie, are you feeling okay? I mean, besides Oma—"

"Dying?"

He sighs, closes his eyes.

Dad frowns, shakes his head. "We need to talk about college, Lu. And the partying. And Marta. Mart's home now. The house is getting full. And Mom. You need to call your mom." His voice trails off, falls quiet, and he presses a thick, shaking hand to his eyes. A tear rolls slowly down his cheek and Miles puts a small palm on Dad's thick shoulder.

I look at him and realize I haven't even tried to absorb what he's going through, losing his mother, his last living parental. *An emotional infant*, I believe, were Marta's words. And it occurs to me again that life, it's ticking on by, all the time. My insides melt and I want to say or do something to help, but before I can get my act together and be a decent human, Dad stands and heels it to the bathroom, Miles close behind. And I'm too late. To give him a hug or tell him how sorry I am. Anything.

I get up, do a gaggle of dishes, and then Zoë's buzzing my speak, reminding me (though she doesn't need to) that the Pennies' toaster is tonight and neither of us are gonna miss it if it's the last flippin' thing we ever do. She says she'll swing by and we can hang for the day, and just as I'm making my not-so-stealthy escape, Marta, looking both well rested and well read, comes sauntering in the front door. I brace myself.

The Cousins are piling in, too, Auntie Julie's little girl, and Auntie Kay's twin boys. Uncle Edgar, Kay's husband, is already getting going on a round of early morning Republican Cross Fire with any left-minded fishy chump enough to bite the lure. And my sister-Jack, no doubt wake-and-baked out of her skull, is eyeing the bait with red-eyed interest.

I slink by the crowd at the door, dodging the free-flying political shrapnel. Between breaths Marta shakes her head, hissing disapproval at me like a slow-deflating tire.

"Be right back, Jacks," I lie and hop down the steps, snag my spin, and start heeling on foot up the hill. Not a moment too soon, Zoë and Gideon are pulling up beside me, Zoë tweaked because I gave such lame-o directions to my Oma's and she got lost three times.

I apologize and load my bike on her rack, settle into the back seat. Up front, Zo and Gid talk low, some major heart-Jack drama boiling in their ever-simmering pot, both of them giving me and my sick-old-person aura a wide berth. I still haven't really spilled to Zoë what's going on, just how serious it is. It hasn't felt right. Or real. I think maybe saying it out loud will make it true, so I don't say anything at all.

Miss Heartbreak Hotel

We sunbathe the day away on Gid's new back patio, and come dusk, we heel it to my empty, echoing house to shower and slap on some proper clothes. I wait around while Zo experiments with about twenty different—though very similar—outfits and I nervously chew my nails and drag a tar out my bedroom window. No more after this one. For real. I go to the bathroom and rinse and repeat with mouthwash and say, unblinking into my own eyes, "No more."

We park at Green Lake and follow the Pennies' hand-drawn, red-crayon treasure map to Clay Beach. Along the narrow wooded path, we throw back searing swigs of Cuervo from the Five-Fingered Flask and we know we approach X marks the spot when we see the flickering bonfire and hear the hollers and squeals of a toaster, sharp in the night.

At the bonfire I put my nose to ground and am hot on the trail of No Longer Miss Ancient History.

"No, Eve's not here," they say. My smile fades.

"She's not coming." My heart sinks.

"Nate and her split." My ears perk.

"She's heartbroken. He was scheming on her with a sophomore." My mind whirls.

"I hear she fainted she was so clash." My heart breaks.

I'm more and more worked up and I talk to Zoë about Eve too much. I'm spewing sentences and I say her name over and over, just to feel the taste of it between my teeth and on my tongue and hear it hit the night air like a shock of electricity. I can't believe Eve's MIA.

Zoë's not concerned. She says, "Go Children Slow, Butler. At least she's finally hit to Nate's scheming. Who cares she's not here?"

So I say, "Not I," and prove it by flirting with the flap-Jack who graduated last year and plays college soccer at a small, crank school in a small, crank town. I'm boisterous and witty and kick his flip butt in a brewcan shotgun showdown and he laughs and thinks I'm a badrat as he high-fives me and hugs me tight.

Eve finally does arrive, Miss Heartbreak Hotel, in late high fashion, and her Pennies are a cooing crowd of overly sympathetic clichés. I wait but it seems I won't be getting a word in edgewise.

"Hey, it's beat! It's beat. Be easy. We patched it up." Eve smiles her electric lips, though her eyes don't follow their cue. "We're switch. We're kill. It was all a massive, mop flip-up." She's reassuring and coaxes her flap-Jacks into sub-dued, sauced submission. They continue to hover around their queen of the hive.

As the hype slowly dies, I realize I've lost my nerve. I go Ophelia and ditch the increasingly sloppy Soccer-Star-Nobody-Man and am paralyzed by what I want. I've waited, impatience twitching under my skin, all day and night for Eve, but now I can't be near her. She's too bright, and I blink and squint and turn away from her comet trail as it moves like fire through the crowd.

I heel it far down the shore and find flat stones that rock and roll my sauced body when I send them skipping, hip hop, across the lake's glassy face. I pee behind a prickly shrub and lie by the shore as my head spins and swims. I'm a sticky little magnet dangling into the vast black sky and I claw the sand to keep from free-falling in.

There's a ruckus as boys with men's voices whoop and holler and I see flecks of splashing water and hear the diving and spraying of bodies hitting liquid in the night. I stand and wobble and giggle as I remember where I am and who is here.

I'm resolute.

I will stand and conquer.

For best results, rinse and repeat.

I am In Pursuit of Miss Heartbreak Hotel.

The Magician

We're sitting on a rock. Eve Brooks and me.

———

I was standing, scatting a group of flap-Jacks, when suddenly she was behind me, grabbing my shoulders and hugging my neck, squeezing my esophagus, saying, "What's eggs, Beatstreet Bug? How's your happyface?"

I coughed, said, "Vise Grip Jones, watch the plumbing!"

as I rubbed my throat and she laughed, sauce thick on her breath.

───────

We're sitting on a rock. Eve is sighing and talking about what a clash mop heart-Jack Nate Gray is. I'm dragging a tar.

I feel her watching me. "That's one toxic hobby you got there," she says. "I thought you were quits."

"You're one to talk."

"Be easy, Bug. Nate's hit," she says. "He just has a lot going on."

I drag. "I hear you passed out."

"Oh." She takes a breath. "I've been eating only grapefruits for a week," and I turn, give her goggle eyes. "I'm on a diet," she says and then schemes a drag from my tar.

"Hypocrite," I say as she hands it back. She smiles, and then chokes. She coughs and smoke billows from her mouth and she's gagging and sticking out her tongue. "I'll catch your lung if you hack it up," I say, leaning into her and cupping my mitts under her chin.

───────

She touched the roughed-up red of my throat and laughed, saying, "If I'm Vise Grip Jones, you are the Magician. You make me laugh when I'm sad. You perform marvelous, death-defying acts of cunning and charm." She didn't really say that, but I would like to think she would have if she hadn't said, "Oh crank, I think I'm gonna be sick."

We ran to the woods and she wasn't sick. Not even a little. She burped a belch that woke the dead natives sleeping below our feet and we hooted and held our shaking brew-filled bellies with glee.

We're sitting on a rock. Eve and I split a piece of gum and she blows tiny snapping bubbles as I pull my hood up over my head and explain my Theory of the Universe. That is: We're all walking talking Popsicle sticks with our heads melting, our brains juice at our feet.

We're sitting on a rock. Eve's superfreeze ace in this speckled white-and-blue angora sweater and I'm studying it, petting it softly like a pup.

"My apple-Jacks are driving me bananas," she says. "It's like school never ended and the drama just goes on." I nod, glad she's confiding in me. "Hey, Beatbug," she sighs. "I wish we could've stayed hit these past years. I really coulda used you by my side. Even if you are a toxic hobbyist, I'm glad we're ponies 'n' pigtails again."

I smile. "You've massive missed out."

Eve laughs. "And so have you."

And she points a finger at my nose and I bat at it like a cat, and she mimes like it hurts.

"True words," I say.

*

We sit on this rock and I tell her about my Oma. Eve picks up a water-smoothed stone and places it, warm from her hand, into mine.

*

We're stumbling up the path to my banger. It's massive dark. "I know these trails," she says. "I grew up in these woods." I picture her here, a miniature version of her now, white-blond curls, red dress, and Mary Janes, dog off its leash, mother and father heeling it arm in arm. They sing a song about a frog and some logs and laugh in fits at the riot parts.

"Your life's like a Disney flick," I say.

"You don't know flip about my life."

"Truth," I say and shut my crank mouth, feel a-flap-Jack.

"Or dare?" she finally says.

"Huh?"

"Truth or dare, Lu Butler?"

I laugh. "Dare."

"Um," she thinks. "Crush all the tars in your pack." I roll my eyes at the night sky and twist and turn the crumpled box, paper and tobacco in my mitt. "Beatstreet." She smiles.

We keep walking, I push a branch from my face. "Truth or dare, Eve Brooks?"

"Truth."

I'm silent. Then I laugh. "Would you or have you ever kissed another betty?"

My question hangs between us like a hammock as we forge ahead. "Nope. Never have. But . . . word. I think I would. Not just any ace-Jack, though. She'd have to be something special." She smiles at me over her shoulder.

I try not to trip.

"Truth or dare, Lu Butler?" she says into the woods.

"Dare."

Eve whips around in the path. "No fair! All you want is dare. No truth." She crosses her arms over her chest.

"Well, word, then. Truth. Probe away, Miss Inquisition. Ask anything." She looks at me for a minute and then shakes her head.

"No." She smiles. "I don't need to ask. I know you and all your pesky Bug secrets."

I laugh. "I'm sure you do," I say, but I'm not so sure she does.

⁘⁘⁘

We're sitting in my banger. *My* heap banger. We. Us. Me and Evelyn Brooks. I'm sliding fast into sober as I start the engine and feel her arm brush light against mine.

She's shivering and chit-chattering and I'm blasting on the heat and wiping the fog off the windshield with my sleeve. I slide out of my hoodie and fork it over to her. She's got freckles on the backs of her hands. She's sleepy and slow and I'm geared up, fully charged. The pulse of my blood under my skin, in my groin, under my temples is overwhelming, deafening. Eve fumbles with her seat belt and says, smiling, with a big yawn, "I'm all thumbs, Bug."

I laugh. "Listen, Thumbs. You could just crashpad at my house tonight," I suggest, the coolest cucumber on the block.

"No, Bug," she says. "I gotta jetset home. I'm early-bird shift at the restaurant tomorrow morning. Plus, you don't understand. I *have* to brush my teeth."

"Word," I laugh and we wheel in silence, tunes slipping softly through our ears, moving so hush through our sleeping town to her front door. She's no longer Ms. Ancient-History-His-Betty-Vise-Grip-Jones. I am no Magician.

And we are Lu and Eve. Bug 'n' Thumbs.

Low Tide

In her driveway, Eve asks if I'm into a glass of water. I nod and follow her in.

In her front hall, she says, "I'll be back," and returns toting two toothbrushes with massive white gobs of paste on their bristles. I laugh, take one.

"This isn't, like, your dog's toothbrush, or anything?"

"We don't have a dog. We have a cat."

We brush side by side at the kitchen sink, her stepdad's snores descending softly through the ceiling. We spit and our frothy white foam whirls side by side down the drain. I steal her hand and wipe my mouth on the frayed cuff of my sweatshirt she's still sporting. "Don't get this all cruddy," I say. "It's my favorite." And she checks me with her hips.

She walks me out and I count twelve steps from the front door to my car, trying to calm my nerves going haywire inside. We stand by the open door and she says, "Thanks for the lift." She begins backing away and my hopscotch heart fissures. She says, "Night," waving a small hand and I've come undone. She walks away and I sink into my car, heart crawling up, clinging to my throat. She turns and heels it back over to me. I climb out.

"Don't wanna forget," she says as she starts sliding out of my sweatshirt.

"Keep it," I say. "It superfreeze fits you. B'sides, I don't give a rat's tail about that crank old thing. It's like shrink wrap me. Makes my arms look like Abraham Lincoln arms. You know, like, crazy, long Abraham Lincoln . . . arms." I hold my bare wrists up massive awkward and she laughs and drops her hands to her sides.

"Oh, pesky Bug, you're very special," she says, laughing. "Does your dad ever tell you that?" I shrug and giggle. Her words from before come back—*she'd have to be something special*—and I wonder.

She walks to my open door and wraps her arms around my neck and my life could end now. Her blond curls are thick and cool with summer nights on my face as I hug her, and when she lets go, she's smiling, big.

I wanna kiss you, I think, but my lips are silent as my heart cage thumps a heavy-metal hair-band double bass drumbeat.

"What's eggs?" she says. "You look massive sad."

"I think . . . I d-dunno," I stutter. I must be unhinged. "This is so flip. But I feel like I'm missing you already." I frown comically. "That must sound so crickets." And we're laughing and she's hugging me tight, again. Her body, so close, again.

We stand and our heads bow together.

"Not crickets," she says softly. "Be easy."

Her face so close.

And then, I'm kissing her.

A small, soft thing of a kiss. An idea. A question. The world's spin stops, sputters, stalls. And then she's pulling away slowly, wide-eyed and smiling, holding her fingertips to her mouth. She shuffles backward and my brain function returns in increments, and I smile, watching as she heels it to her front door, looking over her shoulder at me, her fingers still at her lips. She leans her back into the door, her hands two small peace signs, and then I'm folding into my banger just as my bones turn to dust and I'm washed away in her low tide.

Supercollider

I've dialed and buzzed her many, many times. It's two days since the Kiss Heard Round the World, though the movie trailer version of it plays surround-sound high-def, nonstop, through my flap-happy skull. I've dialed her four too many times.

She's not Call Missed. She's not Call Waiting. She's No New Messages. She's Zero New Buzzes.

She's Not Calling Me Back.

I'm freaking out.

I walk. I jog. I swim. I think about not thinking about dragging tars. I'm in motion. I hear scientists on the news say *supercollider* and I know what they mean.

What I don't do is buzz my apple-Jacks. They buzz and I pounce at my speak, Eve on my mind, but it's never her and I die a little inside. From her messages, I can tell even Maya's beginning to take it personally. Zoë's beyond jammed. In her last buzz she was all, *I'm sending to China for a new, more interactive model of mail-order apple-Jack.* But I can't talk to them. They could crack my little egghead shell and my beans would spill out every which way and then the whole flip world would know that I kissed Eve. They would never understand.

I'm errands-girl extraordinaire around Oma's house, always up for jetting out and snagging this or that, never resting long by her wicker sofa bed—the jitters are back, the sweats, too. Mostly I pick up more double chocolate crunch ice cream for Om, who's either asleep or a massive munchy hippo. I wonder for a minute if Marta isn't sneaking her canna treats of some sort. When I see him around, Dad's all leaning on me about college and figuring out my rooming and preseason situation, and I realize I forgot I was going. How can there be a thing called college when there's a betty called Eve. I pause in my sit-ups and say, "I'm beat, Dad. Can't wait."

I pedal and pump on my spin and remember Eve still hasn't dialed me back. I get home. I run. I do sprints between telephone poles. My nose drips and I spit thick mucus and threads stick to my lips and I wipe them on my sleeve. My lungs burn and my legs are heavy lactic acid logs and I'm hacked and wired and my guts are chock-full of jumping beans hopping their way back to Mexico.

I run and I run and I run.

<hr/>

My counting obsession is ruining my life. The longer Eve doesn't buzz, the more anxious and amped I get, the more I count. I've graduated from the innocent simplicity of counting steps, to spelling out full sentences, ticking off their letters, over and over, in my crank, cracked brain. Phrases loop in my mind, round and round, like a rogue Ferris wheel spun way out of whack. I count and I count. So mop, so OCD. Hello, my name is Lucy Butler and I'm a compulsive letter counter.

Back when Zo and I would roll E for weeks on end, those were my peak Ophelia counting days. The more I rolled, the less I slept. The less I slept, the more I tweaked. The more I tweaked, the more I spelled. Then cut. Sliding blade edges up the inside of my arm or over my hip, across my ribs.

Scratching out words or letters with my fingernails into the back of my hand or inner thigh. It was the only thing I knew could calm me down, mellow me out, hit reset. Totally Ophelia, totally over.

But the letter thing is back. It starts out as a thought, and that repeats, and then I'm spelling out the words, adding spaces and punctuation, until it all fits just so. Right now on rotation is, *she isn't dialing me back*. I tick my fingers, one, two, three, four, five, to check my mental work.

S-H-E-(space)-I-S-N-(apostrophe)-T-(space)-D-I-A-L-I-N-G-(space)-M-E-(space)-B-A-C-K

With no period, it's perfection. Twenty-five ticks. Switch and even. Balanced and orderly. Ahhh. Feel the obsessive-compulsive bliss.

Another phrase comes, after a sharp-tongued call from my sister-Jack wondering where I'm at.

F-L-I-P-(space)-O-F-F-(comma)-(space)-M-A-R-T-A

Fifteen ticks with the comma.

And another pops up at will.

Y-U-P-(space)-I-(space)-K-I-S-S-E-D-(space)-A-(space)-B-E-T-T-Y

Twenty with no comma after *yup*.

I'm tempted to buzz Eve's speak and write:

Y-O-U-(apostrophe)-R-E-(space)-D-R-I-V-I-N-G-(space)-M-E-(space)-O-P-H-E-L-I-A

Twenty-five.

But I don't.

I'm on my spin, pedaling away, zooming up and down hills, thinking about Eve, and high school, and college, and Eve. It's been five days. Five.

Zoë and Maya have each rung about twenty hundred times, and Castle's buzzed twice, and I keep my head down, eyes on the tar. I roll up at Oma's and brake to a stop. I hop off and lean my spin against the old pool area fence, looking out over the once-brimming, chlorine-laden waters now filled in and grassed over, a fertile patch of overgrown green marking its once-rectangular depression. I remember a few years back when Oma had it filled in, after Opa passed, and all us wee-Jacks had gotten too big for summertime days dippin' and divin' in the sunshine. She was crying and I didn't understand why. Now, suddenly, I do.

Swimming lessons, I remember. Being fresh outta kindergarten, popping animal floaty toys with Marta and wearing their skins like hides. Operation Crime Scene—grinding colored chalk along the ridges of our cousins' small, glistening bodies and taking testimonials from Mom and Dad and the aunties asking, *Where were you on the night of August the second?*

The smell of wet tar, strawberries grown by Oma working summer-long, bent at her waist, knee-deep in garlic scapes, lettuce greens, parsley, seed-headed weeds. Eve Brooks and I, in sixth, holding freeze pops to bee stings on the balls of our feet, the tiny, buzzing bodies meeting their makers in the far patch of clover doubling as croquet pitch. Marta sending my ball flying with one crack of her mallet, Eve always taking the extra turn. Badminton tournaments till dusk with the aunts and Mom and Dad drinking down the sun. The good ole days.

I take off my helmet and walk inside, peek my head into Oma's quiet room, push my hand into my hard-pounding heart. Auntie Kay is helping her eat a bowl of chicken noodle. Oma stops, looks up at me.

"Heya, Oms," I say. "Long time no see."

She smiles hazily, nods her head. I take a breath and tread lightly across the carpet, on tiptoes—for no reason whatsoever—and lean over, wrap my arms around her tiny, angular body. She sighs and pulls me into a warm, bony-armed hug, and when I straighten up, Oma's eyes are cloudy, far away. She searches my face.

"How's that sweet girl?" she says. "Your friend, little Evie?" and I laugh at her bizarre mental powers, run my digits along the impossible softness of her hand as I did as a wee-Jack during sleepovers, when she'd read Mart and I stories before bed.

"She's beat," I say. "I'll tell her you say *hey.*"

"Do that," she says, her breathing getting heavy, and Kay gives me a nod. I step aside, watch her help Oma put away a few more mouthfuls of chicken noodle, and then slip away into the clutter and motion of Oma's dimly lit living room.

I fall back onto the couch beside my sister, secretly wipe at the small pool of tears brimming in my eyes. I breathe, slow, again and again, matching the Beeps I hear from Oma's adjacent room.

Marta groans and I look down at the floor where she sits, slumped. She's sulking as another turn of Mille Bornes (our German family's favorite French card game) passes her by, Uncle Edgar gloating, telling me how he's creaming her and his sons with an evil stream of doled out Flat Tires and Stops, a massive, scat-eating grin spread wide across his red, ruddy face. I lean in, scat some trash on Marta's behalf, and finally, after much heated faux-Français banter, Marta gets a Spare Tire. And then a GO. With only fifty miles left to win, Edgar's one-dimensional rig runs outta petro via an Out of Gas from his oldest son and Marta coasts to an easy win.

"Karma's a killer, eh, Ed?" I laugh, and Marta, shuffling the cards, chuckles beside me, leans her shoulder into mine. I can't remember the last time we touched. We look up, see the aunts talking heatedly in the kitchen, and my heart flutters, my chest tightens. The living room goes hush as we listen for the Beep Beep of Oma's pulse.

And it's still there. It sounds and we all remember to breathe.

"She's hanging in," Uncle Ed sighs reverentially, slapping his cards on the floor.

"Another round?" asks Mart.

"Deal me in," I say, and scoot down onto the floor.

Galaxies

Everyone's crashpadded out in the spare rooms, all the lights are low, and I'm downstairs in Oma's musty basement, shifting letter magnets on the icebox's mottled white hide, spelling out the names of as many of her myriad of mysteriously deceased cats as I can manage to remember. Starting with *Twinkle Eyes* on the line down to *Hot Wheels*. So far I have ten. I pull open the sticky door, look inside, scope three mason jars filled with green-colored goo, a Ninja Turtle action figure frozen in each. I laugh 'cause I remember this day, when Marta and the cousin Jacks and I played Turtles Get Cryogenically Frozen and we made Oma whip us up some of her world-famous soap-and-glue slime. We were all having a jolly ole time slopping our Turtles around in their jars of muck when Marta's fell and smashed on the floor and nobody would help her towel up the goo that spread like sticky green lava under the fridge, oozing and conjoining with twenty decades of cat hair and dust and dead bugs. Needless to say, the fun stopped there and we ditched our Turtles in the icebox for later. Or never, as it turns out.

It's massive weird because I'm so horny right now I'm making me uncomfortable. It's literally the last way I want to feel in my Oma's old basement, rifling through her old fridge. And just then, Eve, she finally dials.

"Hey," I say.

"What's eggs?"

Crickets.

"You called back," I finally say, squinting into the glare of the refrigerator light.

"I'm massive sorry. I've been gigging doubles the past few days."

I'm silent.

"You're jammed."

I'm not jammed enough. "I'm . . . it's fine."

More crickets.

"So, the other night."

"Word. I'm sorry about that."

"No," she says quick. "No. Don't be that."

"Oh. Okay. 'Cause I'm not."

And she laughs, miles away. Galaxies rush between us, old airwaves of the first radio shows, stars and planets. Then space. And silence.

"Me neither."

I smile, realizing I'm violently shaking a Ninja Turtle jar in my left hand. I put it down on the counter, watch the condensation pool around the base, smooth down my bangs.

She sighs. "I mean, my apple-Jacks would so flip if they found out." And I know she's right. "And, like, I dunno."

My heart is sinking fast, ballast balls careening down to a dark, ominous ocean floor. "What about that heart-Jack of yours? You gonna spill to him?"

"What heart-Jack?"

"Huh?"

"Turns out that clash-Jack was scheming on me after all."

"I guess maybe I heard that."

"Yeah."

"Sorry."

"No, you're not."

I laugh, and close the icebox door, spell her name with the magnets in all yellow letters. (Space)-E-V-E-(space).

"So," she says.

"So."

We fall hush again.

"Listen. It's not like this has to be some massive big deal," I say.

"Totally. I know."

"I just wanna, like, be near you all the time. Stalk you and sleep in the bushes beside your house and breathe all over the back of your neck when you're getting in your car."

She laughs. "Oh, Beatbug, you really are something special." She sighs into the phone. "What are you doing right now?"

Stupid question.

Linkin' Logs

Eve and I are standing again in her dark kitchen. I'm near coma with nerves and she's giddy and wide-eyed, bouncing Ping-Pong-style off the walls. I know how she feels. I'm superfly in my trusty navy hat, and I play it cool. Cryogenic.

After I help her put away a heap of swanky lawn furniture and take down streamers and a HAPPY GRADUATION sign—the aftermath of a toaster I clearly wasn't invited to—we're raiding her folks' sauce stash and finding too little. Shots on an empty gut and I think we're pretending we're more bombed than we are. We heel it upstairs and I know she's waiting for me to do something. Anything. But I'm arctic stone. Paralyzed.

A lava lamp glows against terra-cotta-painted walls and I read and reread song lyrics pinned to her wall, each one scrawled out in multicolored marker designs on paper tacked between magazine photos of giraffes and rivers and trees. I stand and spin some tunes on her old turntable. She plugs in white Christmas-tree lights that wind in looping shapes along her walls and ceiling. I scan a shelf of beat glass orbs—glorified paperweights—bubbles and streaks of color blown and frozen into their clear bellies. I pick one up, put it down.

"Word, Thumbs. These are eggs."

Eve smiles and blazes up some incense. I sneeze, wish I had some canna.

We're standing in the middle of the room and I yank on a string of beads hitched to a fan above my skull and the blades whir slowly to life. I watch them going round and round and then Eve's humming crank bad to some Etta, taking a swig of tepid Southern Comfort. I close my lids. I'm thinking about a tar.

Just then a warmth—her breath on my face comes quick and hot, syrupy with sauce. Then her mouth's on mine. Her lips are wet.

She envelops my lower lip, pulling slightly, with a soft

pressure, and her teeth, biting lightly. I open my mouth a crack and her breath head-on collides with mine, and I'm flooded full by her nectarous, boozy air.

Time stops. All clocks are still, wouldn't dare tick. Or tock.

Down, deep into my lungs, I inhale our kiss and she travels light speed through my body and pushes, fiery hot and scorching, into my fingers and toes.

The very tips of our tongues touch, and then push. And pull. We're Slip 'n Slide, we're dancing. Then she's gone, as quickly as she came. I pull open my lids and all I see is her face. Her fingers press tiny scallops into her shining strawberry lips, and her eyes are massive wide, but then the corners of her mouth curl and she smiles.

She's giggling, blinking, and a massive grin hits me fast and furious. She's cracking up as she sits back down on her bed and I sit, too, rubber, like Gumby, and the edges of our hands touch. I curl my pinkie around hers. Linkin' Logs.

I remember: inhale, exhale, inhale, exhale. I yank off my navy hat and stuff it into my skinnies' back pocket. She sighs and drags her hand over her curly golden hair and I'm waxing full again and shining bright. I look smack into her eyes and she laughs, opening her mouth to speak, and I kiss her.

I kiss her. And I kiss her. And I kiss her.

Tag, You're It

I wake up in Eve's bed, feeling strange, somehow split right up the middle. Like half of me is here, and the other half—quiet and alone—is lost, but somewhere near. Across town, the steady Beep Beep of time ever echoing in my ears.

I pull Eve's arm off my chest and shimmy out of her sheets. I'm remembering how we went quiet after talking for hours, side by side, my mitt propped under my skull as she nestled in, her head on my heart cage. I was shocked she wasn't thrown across the room by my fast-pumping heart. Ba-boom, ba-boom.

And now here I am, up and heeling it out. Silent, as she sleeps.

I motor over to Oma's, the cold wheel strange under my clammy digits, the heater pumping dank wind into my tired eyes. I slink into the drive, tail between my legs. In her bed, Eve's waking up, thinking I'm there. But I'm not. I'm here, and as the familiar, deathly silence descends, I couldn't regret it more.

***

Oma has a rough go the next day and night and things are feeling massive bleak in the a.m., so Mart and Miles and I heel it to the grocery to give the aunts and Dad some space. I haven't dialed Eve, and she hasn't dialed me, and at the deli counter I start to cry and my sibling-Jacks think it's 'cause of Oma and I'm not so sure it isn't.

"'Emotional infant' is the phrase I think you're looking for," I say, Miles taking my hand, but Marta just smiles. A rare bird.

"It's so flip, Lu, 'cause the last time I came here that's exactly what I did," and I laugh at the cold glare of fluorescent lights and slabs of dead animal, sad and happy to my core, and start blubbering all over again. They escort me to the truck, where we binge on Oma's double chocolate crunch and get massive coma on sugar.

Back home, I dial Zoë, the words, the story of Eve and me, at the tip of my tongue. But Zoë's all steamed, saying, "What thinkhole you fall down, thithta-Jack? We thought you'd detherted the troopth!"

"Thtop that," I say, working to play along. "You know I couldn't thurvive without you," and I tell her I've been buried deep dealing with the situation with Oma.

"Um, what situation?" she says, and I spill the whole, ugly scoop. Zoë can't really stay mad at me after this and tells me the Cats Plus Gid are meeting at the Falls for an early morning swim and I tell her I'm in.

At the shore, our Fools Band of Four ditch our shoes, shorts, and hoodies and wade in, the cold water streaming up to our bathing suit bottoms. Gideon jives about shrinkage and Zoë and I jive about him jiving about shrinkage. The rocks are slick-rick sludge coated until we get closer to the base of the falls, where freshwater fish with translucent green and pink scales dart between pockmarked gray boulders and smooth, iron-colored stones. The waterfall leaves its bed ten feet above where we stand and the liquid pounds thick over the rift. A lion of a falls, it foams and smacks and roars. We shout to each other but our voices are lost. We're all a whoop and hollering and playing tag-you're-it with the spray.

I'm the first to stick my skull under. The falls tug at my neck and I yelp and heel it back, tossing my dripping shag. I squat by the cascade and submerge massive slow and soon I'm beneath it, the torrent crashing cymbals onto my head and shoulders and legs and the volume of the world is flipped to nil as the surge of water engulfs me and I'm pelted until I'm near coma and numb. I think of Oma and wish in an aching rush she could do something like this, get outta that creaky cot and dingy room and remember what life feels like, *really*, pulling and yanking and tearing at your skin and head and limbs.

And in a moment of reckoning, I realize I'm terrified of what I've always wanted and maybe now could have. I'm terrified. It's so simple. I emerge gasping and sputtering in the heavy glare of the sun, and the ruckus of the easy wooded world is deafening and exuberant and raw.

And I love this clawing, screaming, tormenting life. I love this life of mine.

Soft Suns

I lay out on the grass of the old swimming pool and I snag my speak, buzz Eve a few lines I've composed and edited over and over in my head.

Sorry I bailed. Way lame. If u aren't 2 busy plotting my death and/or sticking pins in ur voodoo doll of me, u should come by. Oma was just asking bout my little friend Evie.

I stare at my screen and wait. I wonder where she is, what she's doing, who she's with. The sun is massive hot. Too hot. Oppressive. I pull out a sweaty grocery receipt from my pocket and jot down a poem that comes quick to my mind. A crank sad stab at an apology.

> *I left before the sun. But*
> *just after the moon. So no one could see*
> *or tell about*
> *the half girl in her half body,*
> *crumpled in her half hand a*
> *kiss, goodbye*
> *unleft and unremembered*
> *for half-true reasons*
>   *even half girls will never truly know.*
> *—I'm sorry.*

I fold up the paper and tuck it deep down into my pocket. I squirm and wait. I'm a sticky little gummy worm wriggling in the dirt and I burrow my toes through the grass and into the cool top layer of soil. The cicadas' hum is a 360-degree dissonant symphony in my ears. I'm drowning in this mess of me.

Finally, Eve buzzes back.

Be there in ten.

Bull's-Eye

"Really, I'm sorry I bailed." We're sitting on the warm stone wall overlooking the old badminton field. Below our feet, busy bees scurry in white clover.

"I get it," Eve says, the midday sun glowing her profile a golden blaze.

"I mean it. And then I used my Oma to get you to heel it over here and now she's asleep." Eve laughs, looks at me with one eye closed to the light.

"She's probably not even sick," she says, shoving my

shoulder, and my pulse jumps as I'm snagging her hand, my fingers curling into hers. My armpits and knees erupt in sweat.

"No, she is," I manage to say.

"I know."

I climb down the wall monkey-style, showing off, and we wander through the yard and scope a jumble of bright green three-speed Schwinn spins stashed away in Oma's musty shed for what must be eons. Swooping handlebars, leather saddles, and red-rusted shifters that sit at a massive cricket angle on the top tube frame and I say let's take a ride but Eve says these bad boys aren't going anywhere. I move through Opa's relic of a workshop like an old pro, show Eve the ancient tools, aged wood grooved in the shapes of his thick, strong hands. And then I get down to tinkering. She watches as I pump full a flat.

"It's hit these ole tires are filling. I was for sure the inner tubes would be wasted."

She crinkles up her nose. "Inner tubes?"

Next I fiddle with her spin's chain that hangs like loose teeth and she's standing, scoping from over my shoulder. The fabric of her flannel is brushing against my back.

"Those things are massive filthy."

"It's grease, Jack."

"Grease?" And I smile.

I show her what's an Allen wrench and how to squirt a can of WD-40 and tighten a bolt and realign the brakes.

"Beatbug?" she says, and I look up, a black smear running a line from her freckled nose to her ear. I drop my wrench to stand, wipe her face with the cuff of my sleeve.

"Yeah?"

"When did you know you were into betties?"

"Oh," I say. "I . . . dunno. I guess I've always known. Ever since my first crush, way back when."

"Way back when *when*?"

"Kindergarten, maybe. Does that count?" She nods, slides her fingertips into the front pocket of my jeans, and my skin is live wires, hot circuits. I play it cool. "But I've always been massive stiff scared to do anything about it. No matter how much I wanted to, I just never did. Never thought I could."

"Hmm," she hums, stepping back to snag a ball of twine, twirling one end round and round her finger. "You weren't stiff scared with me."

I laugh. "I was! Sure as shootin' I was. I'm still sorta yeller. You ain't?"

She shrugs. "Not with you. You don't spook me, Beatstreet Butler. You're sugary as peach 'n' cream pie, ponies 'n' pigtails galore."

"Me?" I mock horror. "I'll have you know I'm the most meanest, most durn tootin,' most gun-totin'-est, most hard-knockin'-est flap-flippin'-Jack in these here parts. Heart a' stone, thas Bull's-Eye Butler."

"Sure," she says. "Whaver you say, Bull's-Eye," and I laugh, squat beside the spins to finish up.

"All right, Thumbs." I stand, wiping my hands on an old, dirty rag. "Let's roll."

"Y'know, I forgot you're so gosh-dang handy, what with all this tinkerin'. It's pretty dang hot." And I'm grinning flap-Jack big and massive wanna jump all up in her bones.

———————————

Twenty minutes later Eve and I are happyface riding our switch old spins on the rail-trail when Eve grins mischief, chug-chugging quick ahead.

"Go Children Slow," I warn. "These ole beasts can't shred gravel the way they used to."

She cranes her neck and smiles back, pedaling faster still. Then her handlebars get wobbly, and bump bump she goes, over a tree root and a bolt in her seat snaps clean and she's careening from the path, rodeo-style through the trees. Her spin's chain catches fast on a stump and it shoots off the gears and she's grinding to a gut-wrenching stop.

Her shoulders are shaking as I roll up, worrywart central.

"What's broken?" I say, skidding out and dashing to her side.

And then I see she's laughing riots, and when she scopes my flipped mug, she says, "Look at you, Bull's-Eye Butler, hard-knockin', flap-flippin', heart-a'-stone-Jack."

She's laughing so hard even I crack a small smile. *"Rinse and repeat*, Bug. I didn't break. Not even close," and she drops her cranked-up spin to the ground. The seat gives another groan and crack and she's a flip-flop howling hyena again.

"Oh, word, Thumbs," I say, kick at its tire. "Massive riot. But what Popsicle stick's gonna tinker this in-n-out heap?"

She smiles. "You?"

"Nope. *We.*" And I poke her in the ribs and she wraps her arms around my neck and my legs turn to jelly but I don't buckle or sway. I pull her hard into me under the soft rustle of woodsounds and birdsong and we stand there breathing into the other, my whole being electric with her touch. A mom pushing a stroller comes jogging by, so we quickly peel ourselves apart and heel it home to tinker the chain and seat together. Bug 'n' Thumbs.

———

We're just finishing up in the garage, the sun cresting high in the sky, when Dad, Mart, and Miles pull in with a truck full of grub. We help them lug it in and I roll my eyes as Dad grills Eve on her post–high school plans, on college, career, and the great beyond.

I tell him to lay off, but Eve, she's radiant and eloquent and has it all figured out: the Master Plan. I cut in, asking if she's set up a 401(k), or preregistered for any retirement communities in the Florida Keys. Dad just laughs, slaps a palm to his forehead, and announces he's upgrading his Daughter Plan, thinks he can get a good trade-in rate at the store. Good ole Marta goes splitting a gut at this until she remembers she's also his daughter and then she's throwing a small fit. She stalks off into the living room and Dad gives me a funny look when I say I'm gonna drive Eve home, so probably won't be back around until late.

"*What?*" I say, furrowing my brow.

"Nothing," he says. "Nothing at all."

But I don't believe him.

Centipedes

Eve and I decide to heel it quick down to the lake before the sunset and I shadow her steps as we twist and turn down trails. She's a light woods walker and a massive flip whistler, but does it anyway. I laugh and mimic her wayward melodies and we toot and flute our way to the water's murky edge. Hot pine needles and swampy sludge and slime are in my nose and I inhale deep.

"Smells like centipedes."

"Centipedes?" she says, eyebrow cocked, curly hair aflame.

"Word, flap-Jack. What's so flip 'bout that?"

"Dunno," she laughs. "I didn't know centipedes smelled like anything."

"They do! Behind our old shack in the city, under Mom's lilacs, there were these cold, mossy rocks that, like, a gajillion centipedes lived under, just whirlwinding their crank little legs away. And it smelled just like this."

Eve catches my eye. "You don't really talk so much about your mom anymore."

"Not much to scat. Just that she's gone." I walk a few steps, feel the place inside me that holds her—small, hard, sharp. "Her choice, not mine. I try not to be jammed at her for heeling on us. Just dial on Christmas, Thanksgiving, say *hullo*. Whatever."

She sighs. "That's very evolved of you. If my mom jetset to start another life with other Jacks . . ."

"Yeah, well, Marta kept beating me out for Most Angry Award, so for the past three, four years I've been working Indifference pretty hard. It's going well."

She laughs. "I see."

"And anyway, those goddamn rocks of hers with the goddamn centipedes, they smelled just like this."

Eve steps forward, clutches my earlobes with her warm digits, and she kisses me in a patch of sun like a hummingbird on a lilac. Nose to nose, forehead to forehead, bumper to bumper.

"Your mom shouldn't have jetset on you," she whispers. "Shouldn't have in a million years." And I press my eyes closed, willing tears not to come, but they do. We stand and she holds me, and the moments tick by only for us.

"I'm a mess," I mumble and then she's smiling, nipping at my nose, and I poke her in the ribs, growl, and she hoots, spinning on her heels. I wipe my sad-sack face and lope after her down the worn and winding path. Nothing should feel this good.

"That does *not* smell like centipedes," she says as we round a corner to the lake onto a large stone outcropping. The air's pungent with canna and we're suddenly standing above a gang of five red-eyed smiling-Jacks I know so well.

Dream Queen Raine with Mister Blue Eyes, and three other party hardies peer up at us and say, "What's beat, Butler!" and Eve and I shimmy and shake down the rocks. Eve's hush as I scat with Raine and Blue and I can see Eve's not hit with these Jacks. I introduce her and they scope her massive skeptic but then Blue says, "Eve Brooks. Nate Gray's girl, yeah?" and Eve laughs sorta crickets, shakes her head.

"They're spilt," I say. "Banana split," and everyone nods

their heads, like Eve being split with Nate makes her A-OK to crashpad their powwow.

We take hits of their harsh canna and soon I'm laughing and squinting into the lake's glimmering glare, befuddled and full of stupid, mindless joy. I'm linking nets with Blue, who's cracking me up, thinking for sure he saw a whole family of beaver swim by, when Raine busts in and pulls me away and slings an arm around my shoulder.

"Well, the rumors are true," she says, and my mug's massive hot and glowing as I sling my own heavy arm over her. And it suddenly feels so normal. Raine Hall feels okay.

"Pigs can fly? I know. But, they need two seats and don't fly as much as they used to."

"Wow," she laughs. "That was ... *creative*. But no, wee-Butler. My ship's a-sailin'. I'm jetset in a week. Off to the great unknown! Well, the Cayman Islands."

"Man-o, Jack! But what in tarnation'll you do without me or this hog-killin' town?" and she's giggling, her head tipped toward mine.

"Well, I dunno 'bout this rathole dump, but you could stow away as first mate. Mend sails, bum smokes, hit canna in the sun, sauce on brews, and dip-skinny. What more could a betty-Jack want?"

"Solid ground." I grin, stomping my feet. "'Ain't flip in life worth doin' if it cain't be done from a horse,' I always say. I'm Bull's Eye Butler, lily-bellied mainland-lovin' flap-Jack, and I ain't too blowhard t'admit it." I look back grinning at

Eve and she rolls her eyes. "Too far?" I ask. She kicks at a rock.

Raine tosses back her head, cracking up. "You're so Ophelia, Jack."

"Certifiable."

Then another canna's passed, but Eve shakes her head and I know she wants to jetset. I try to catch her eyes but she darts her gaze to the lichen-laden rock. I say, "Word," to everyone and Raine and I have a quick hug. She sticks her digits in my speak, tells me to dial if I can find a pair of adult-sized arm floaties as Eve and I heel it up the trail.

As we walk, Eve's hush and heels it quickly ahead. She stumbles on a root and I catch her but she yanks away her hand.

"Hold it, Jack," I say. She stops but doesn't turn around.

"What?" she asks the trees.

"What's broken, Thumbs?"

"Nothing."

"Right," I say. I put my hand on her hip and she shifts her weight on her feet. She turns her head slightly over her shoulder.

"It's, like, you were trying so hard."

"Me?"

"And she was, like, drooling all over your crank flap-Jack jokes."

"Um."

"Dippin' skinny?" she says, eyebrows raised.

"Dippin' skinny?"

She shakes her curls and turns to face me. "I'll spell it out. You, Jack, were massive flirt with that flap-Jack, Raine Hall. And she was massive flirt with you."

I nod slowly. "O-kay."

"Okay, what?"

"Okay, maybe that's a little bit truth. But, I'm curious, which one jams you most?"

She sticks out her chin, enraged. "Both!" she says, tossing her hands in the air and I can't help but laugh. "What could possibly be riot right now?"

"You."

"Me."

"You, Jack, are jealous."

"Am not."

"Am, too. And it's making you Ophelia-pants."

"No," she says. "It's Raine and her massive phony-Jack vibe that's driving me *Ophelia-pants*, or whatever. And you, Bull's-Eye Butler, pulling that phony cowboy-Jack scat with her!"

"You love when I scat cowboy-Jack!"

"Yeah—to me!"

"Brooks, you are so massive green-eyed. Admit it!"

"No," Eve says again. She turns away from me and brings her fingers to her lips. "Fine," she finally says. "Maybe I am green-eyed. Happy?"

"Most definitively," I say and wrap my nets around her

waist and push my nose into her swan-song neck. She tilts her head onto mine and I'm laughing into her coiled amber shag.

"I got jealous," she says, pouting big, as she turns to face me and I touch my nose to hers and kiss her sad mouth. I kiss her again. She finally smiles.

"I s'pose this means you're really beatstreet for me."

"I s'pose it maybe does." She frowns. "I also s'pose this means you're gonna stop being flirt with flap-Jacks like Raine Hall?"

"Durn tootin'," I say. "Cuz you're my cowgirl, and me, I'm yours," and she laughs out loud and kisses me something fierce. I hold her tight and Eve, she curls into me like a gently closing flower.

Jive

A hop and a skip later and we're skating light along the end of the darkening path, laughing our skulls off about massive dragonfly sex happening all over kingdom come, when we crashpad into two of her *flapple*-Jacks in the parking lot. Pretty Penny One and Two. This town is just too dang small.

"Clash," Eve whispers and they wave and beep beep the remote lock on their massive swank whip.

"Word, *EB*!" They're both superfreeze flip in shades so

massive, their frames swallow their mugs and in their lenses, Eve is tiny, wavering and warped.

"Word, Jacks," Eve says, sporting a fashion of smile she's never worn with me.

"Geezuschrist! Evelyn Brooks! Where the flip've you been all our life?" they say. Their shags are immaculately combed and they sport slinky sarongs with long strands of bathing suit ties looped and bowed at every corner of their bony, tanned bodies.

"Dunno, sweet-Jacks," Eve says. "I've been gigging at the restaurant a ton."

"You should dial us or something. We dialed your speak like a *gajillion* times," they say. "We have to get into it before we all jetset for colley." They both tote massive billowing purses with snaps and buckles and bulges and fringes, strapped with thick bands that drape over their gaunt shoulders.

"Word," Eve says, faking a frown. "I wasn't hit to your dials. My speak's, like, crank, or something. It's been acting massive flip." Just then Eve's speak rings and she yanks it from her pocket, hits ignore. Their eyebrows arch. I laugh. I cough. I shuffle my feet. I'm a parody of a flap-Jack in a massive crickets jam. I back away toward my banger.

"Um," they say. *"So clash."*

We all stand in silence. Eve's speak rings again and she giggles, like popcorn popping. She presses buttons but it keeps ringing.

"Flip," she laughs. "Ponies 'n' pigtails!"

"She's All Thumbs, flap-Jacks," I say, cracking up and Eve snorts, rubbing her watering eyes.

The Pennies drop their pointy chins and scrunch up their noses. "Are you . . . *fried*?" they say, lifting their lenses to look into Eve's red-rimmed eyes. She just shrugs and my sides are aching. "Whatever," they hiss and spin and heel it to their whip, their colorful sarongs wafting like garish enemy flags.

"Rinse and re—" I start to say, but Eve grabs my peace sign fingers and drags me to my car.

We get in and sit and I'm still massive giggling. Eve says stop, so I do. She says, "You don't understand. They're just acting like clash cogs. They're not that flip."

I nod.

"There's just some rules, is all." She flips down her mirror. "And I'm breaking like six thousand and fifty-seven of them—so they're jammed. And they should be."

I nod again.

I watch her mug in the mirror and our eyes meet. She slides on sparkly lip gloss and pulls a fingertip under her eyes. "I haven't dialed, I haven't been into it with them in, like, weeks. I'm not acting like an apple-Jack."

I nod again.

She sighs and flips the mirror back up. "I know what you're thinking, and I don't mean, 'acting'—like *pretending*. I'm a superbeat apple-Jack. I mean, usually, just not lately."

I nod again.

"Listen," she says. "You may think they're clash cogs, but they've been my best Jacks for years. We've had massive good times. And *do not* nod your flip skull again, Bug-Jack!"

I don't nod. I shrug.

"You're driving me *Ophelia*," she mumbles as she grabs the keys from my hand and turns them in the ignition of my car. I pull out of the lot and we cut a wheel and drive in silence.

"And y'know what?" Eve says after many quiet moments. "I don't think I like that word."

"Eh?"

"Lesbian," she says. The L-Bomb.

"That's random."

She sighs, looks out her window.

"I mean, that's what they're gonna call us, you know? If they find out."

I shrug, keeping cool. "Who cares. If people wanna jive, let 'em jive."

"Come on, Bug. You can't scheme you haven't thought about this."

We stop at a red light and I pick at an old sticker of a kitten in a party hat peeling off my dash. "You know I have, Thumbs. But what I'm saying is I don't give a rat's tail about what other clash-Jacks want to call or not call me. Who cares?"

"So, I suppose you've already told Zoë and Maya all about us swapping spit, getting cozy."

I shrug. "That's not what I'm saying."

"Well, forget other Jacks, then. Just for you. Don't you care what this means? Don't you wanna be ready to deal with it when everyone finds out?"

"All I know is I like you. Well, not so much right now—" I check, but she's not smiling. "B'sides, even if Jacks did talk about us, don't you think they'd just find it massive fascinating? I would."

She groans. "You don't know my Jacks. And besides, maybe I don't wanna be massive fascinating."

"Word, Thumbs. Because I hear boring's the new black." She's still not smiling.

"I think you should be more serious about this."

"I'm serious as a broken phalange, beaver fever, Alektorophobia. Just 'cause you disagree with me 'bout this doesn't mean I'm not serious."

"Well, I s'pose that just makes you a better person than me."

"Perhaps. But that's besides the point. I'm just saying, can't we just enjoy ourselves for half a nanosecond without worrying if the flipping world's gonna come to an end? This is fun, right? You and me? Bug 'n' Thumbs?"

She shakes her head. "A girl's gotta think about her future every once in a while, Jack."

"But that's all you do! And, y'know what? Flip it! Flip it all. My Oma's laid up in her bed right now, *dying*. And here we are. *Alive.* And maybe I've just had more time wanting this than you, but I'm not ready to let some flip-flap Barbie-Jacks tell me what I can and can't do."

She sighs, sits back in her seat. I got nothing more. I make like a tree. I'm stumped.

"Eve, what else do you want me to say?"

"That I'm not a lesbian."

"I can't say that. Only you can."

"Word," she says. "I know." And we go quiet again. "What's alektorophobia?"

"Fear of chickens."

She finally smiles.

Soft-Bodied Aphid

Eve hasn't dialed in twenty-four hours and I'm trying not to read too far into it. We've gone longer without talking. Marta, Miles, Auntie Gail, and I are in Oma's kitchen, cooking up a hippie dinner of nut burgers and baby kale salad. Marta's a happy little Betty Crocker and Miles is just about dying from excitement, sandwiched between his two older sisters. After we eat, while the aunts and Dad sit in the kitchen going over and over a stack of forms, the cousins and Uncle Edgar gather for another round of Mille Bornes.

After six decidedly non-karmic rounds, I declare Mille Bornes my least favorite game of all time and leave in a massive funk and go into Oma's room to say an early good night. The aunts come in, say it's time they upped her morphine. I sit in the rocker in the corner of the room and Miles comes in and climbs into my lap and he smells sweet and sticky, like little kid. Everyone else trickles in and drags up an ottoman or folding chair.

Oma's in a lot of pain, the aunts say. She'll be less and less aware, could be any day, any hour, any moment. The more morphine she gets, the closer she is. Which we already knew.

And we all just sit, watching Auntie Gail slide clear liquid from vial into tube, just like the Hospice-Jacks showed. One more dose. Getting closer all the time. And we listen to Oma breathe.

Ten people, in a room, listening to one.

In, out, in, out, in . . .

───────

I dial Eve. She gets home from gigging and doesn't dial me. She has dinner and doesn't dial me. The sun sets and she doesn't dial me. It's late and I finally get her on her home speak.

"Oh, word, Lu."

"Word."

"I never dialed you back. I was gonna after I ate."

"Okay."

"I can't really scat. My mom and I are about to chow." I hear a shaver's voice in the background and Eve goes crickets. "Oh," she finally says. "Word. My step-Jack's here, too. We're just about to sit."

I hear the shaver's voice curse as a pan clanks and Eve's breath comes and then goes hush. She's covering the mouthpiece.

"Are you for sure that's your step-Jack?"

"No. I'm not for sure."

I'm silent.

She sighs. "Nate's here."

I go flip inside. I see in my mind's eye Nate Gray working his shiny-toothed Cheshire cat grin, his sky-blue eyes honing in on Eve, slimy words coiling about, oozing poisonous charm, working his evil magic.

"Oh," is all I manage to say.

"We're just scatting. We're really *just* talking." Her voice rises an octave with each sentence. "Lu, I need to do this. I gotta do this myself. Please."

I shake my head, but she can't see.

"Just trust me. I gotta see this through."

"I'm coming over."

"Don't you dare." Her voice cuts like a knife.

She's soft-bodied aphid and I'm all chewed up.

I hang up and my speak doesn't ring.

Man Down

I'm spiraling. Flip-flop-flapping. Massive.

The whole crank thing slams me like a careening snowplow to the guts and I hole up in Oma's cellar. Like one of her dead and done ghost cats, I prowl, slow and coma, haunting again the cold, mildewed dungeons. I find a sixer of Auntie Kay's Coronas in the fridge and chug-a-lug the brew, and when I think of Nate and Eve, my heart splats and shatters.

I sift through Oma and Opa's old drawers, find a lifetime supply of Old Spice and a secret stash of Reese's Pieces. I shuffle about, sloshing back brews, munching stale candy, looking at the many hanged paintings, mostly done in a hasty, thick-stroked style by Uncle Remmy—my dad's once twin—who died before I was born. I stuff my face with handfuls of sugary, peanutty bits and check behind every dusty cabinet door. I find a slide rule, a horde of pre-sharpened No. 2's, graphing paper, and an old fold-up yardstick. Piles of massive ugly fabrics, scratchy cheap yarn, needles and pins and a little, red-and-black stuffed cushion like a ladybug.

On Opa's old drafting table, I see Marta's initials are carved just under Opa's blocky scratch. I scrape mine in with the tip of an industrial-sized diaper pin, run the edge along the thin skin of my wrist, up my arm a few times, a few times more. Leave a visible series of thin red lines. Stupid. Something I haven't done in a while. But I can breathe again. It does the trick, always.

I switch on the static of an old radio and the faint noise of Oma and Opa's favorite ole-timey jazz crackles and hums.

And my soul grinds to sand. I exhale and am blown away to dust.

To ashes, and back again.

I drag tar after tar out an open cellar window, shivering in my smoke plume as the whole house sleeps, quiet as a lifetime. A deep chill creeps into me from outside and over the cold, tiled floor, eventually ushering me away to the warmth of upstairs. An invisible force leads me past open, dark doorways, Jacks fast asleep, dead to the world. Like a phantom, I wander, zigzag-style into Oma's room, past her old, dusty dresser, glaring white porta-toilet, the Night Nurse snoring quietly in her chair.

She startles as I sit, the old rocker creaking under me and the weight of my heavy heart.

"Sorry," I cringe.

"Oh," the nurse mumbles, blinking open tired, heavy eyes. "I must have dozed off." I never noticed how young she is. Thirty, maybe less.

"S'okay," I say, turning back to Oma. I cough, then burp. "No harm, no foul."

She shifts, and straightens. After a moment, she speaks again.

"You mind if I pop out? I need to make a call. My little girl's been fighting a fever." She looks at me. "You're okay, right?"

I nod, even though I'm so clearly not. She stands, says something about pain, morphine, tube. Needle. Syringe. Something. Fill to, what? First line? Whatever. I nod again.

And I sit. I really am kinda drunk.

I watch my sleeping, dying Oma and the heavy slack of

her jaw and I listen to the thick sucking of her lower lip as she breathes in and out, in and out. It's at this moment I realize she's brave. Infinitely so.

I cross my arms and pull my shoulders up, nearly touching my ears. I rock the chair, back and forth, back and forth.

And Oma, she breathes in and out, in and out. She mumbles softly in her sleep and I turn my head to watch the night creep between the leaves of a dogwood tree that push branches heavy with delicate, flying-saucer blossoms into the glass of the closed window.

I hiccup, giggle, then start to cry.

And slowly, raindrops blink before me on the window and I scope an apparition of myself heeling it up the back hill, smoke trailing like the string of some beheaded balloon. That other half of me, pre-Eve, long gone, gone for long. Far away.

Goodbye.

I hold up tar-stained digits and wave.

Goodbye.

A sudden catch in Oma's beeps snags my ear and I jump, realize I must have dozed off. I watch her and she's still, breathing softly. I sit back.

I take a deep breath. Her eyelids twitch, and suddenly, they shoot open and then shut again. She frowns and her fingers grip the sheets. Forehead creasing, hard. In pain.

I stare for one stupid, stunned second and then stumble over, grab her hand, her too-cold hand and those knuckles, going white, white. Gripping mine. She gasps, her head tilting back and my heart is in my chest and the ten pounds of corn-syrup-chocolate surprise is quick coming up hot tubes, into the back of my throat. And then my speak, it's ringing. Ringing. RINGING. I can't think, I answer.

"Flap-Jack, you're alive!" Zoë's voice comes like a gunshot through the earpiece and I'm a bumbling fool, grabbing at tubes, wires. Bitsy comes bounding in and leaps up into Oma's lap, whimpering, digging softly with her paw at Oma's too-thin thigh, looking to me with watery, alien-dog eyes.

"Zo!" I bark. "Holy crank. Oma, she's—"

"Butler, you sound weird. What's what?"

"Zoë, I'm totally tweaked. She needs her meds and the nurse is somewhere, I dunno. And I just don't remember. Holy goddamn crank, Zo! Her Beep Beeps are all over the place!" I grab a tube of clear liquid from the table, remembering the nurse. *Morphine, needle.* What else?

Pain.

"Butler, are you for serious, right now?" Zoë says. "Are you sauced? Are you strung out? Did you take something? What the flip is going on?"

"Jack, I dunno! I dunno a goddamn thing!" I stare at Oma's face, contorting, twisting. "Ah! What am I doing? What was I just doing?" I remember. "This! I'm doing this," and I focus down at my hands, shaking, shaking, and I plunge the needle tip into the vial of meds, suck up the magic juice. Oma's face contorts in pain.

"How much, Zoë? How much?"

"Are you for real? What'd the nurse say?"

"Something, something, like. Ah—" Something, but what? First? First line?

And I'm lifting the IV connector tube by Oma's arm, the one that goes to the needle sunk down deep in that dark blue vein, the one I've watched the aunts and Dad shoot a dozen times. "I'm gonna shoot the meds, Zo. I gotta."

"Lu, holy crank. Are you sure? Where the flip is your dad?"

"Zoë!" I yell. "I don't know. But she needs this *now*. Okay? Okay. Here I go," and through tremors of biblical magnitude, I guide my two earthquake hands, the needle sliding, sticking, then slipping finally into its connector and my thumb, it slowly depresses the syringe. Bitsy gives a little yelp as Oma takes another gulp of air, her face a map of agony.

And then, and then . . .

"Lu?" The line crackles and Zoë's still there. Oma's eyelids, they flutter open, find my eyes. Then, then, they relax. They close and go slack and Oma, she's sighing a great big groan and her head is sinking soft into her hospital bed pillow. I wait. I listen. I watch.

Beep . . . Beep . . . . . . Beep. It slows.

And my face is going numb, my arms, limbs, fingers,

buzzing from life. Like a snuffed-out candle. Going going gone.

"Holy Mary Jesus," I barely whisper, my whole frame collapsing forward, my head falling into the gristly mass of Bitsy's little body, my speak dropping from where it was pinned between my ear and shoulder. I breathe deep in her dry, doggy scent and then her soft little licks pepper my face, my forehead, my ears. I shiver all over and drip sweat from every single pore at the exact same time.

Then there's a hand on my back and when I straighten up, the nurse, her dark brown eyes are fixed on mine. Bright, shimmering spots speckle her face. I blink through them, but they won't go away.

"No harm, no foul," I hear myself mumble, my speak vibrating in Oma's lap and I fish it out from within Bitsy's curled up joints. And then I'm shuffling through the kitchen and out the front door.

It slams behind me and in blinking stop-motion, I'm stumbling, sliding down the steps and the spots, they go bigger, bigger still. A buzzing, deep and loud, like a swarm of green flies around my head, like pesky beach flies. Like that day at the beach, with Eve. And the stinking white ray. And *What's eggs* in the sand. And I manage two steps, then a third and then I'm aloft, too soon finding ground. I'm Man Down. On the tar I fumble with fingers like marshmallows for my speak, for Eve's number. I need to call her but my chest is clenching and my lungs collapse and there's a scrape of rubber on tar, the slamming of a car door. And someone's face fading in, just there before my own, just as I'm going down, down, down.

Then everything, it all goes black.

I hear my name, and then nothing.

Nothing.

Power Wash

There's water, tiny beads of rain, drip-dropping onto my face.

I open my eyes, and tiny beads of rain are drip-dropping on my face.

I don't remember who I am, or where or when, as tiny beads of rain are drip-dropping on my face.

The sky's trickle joins in a burbling brook of tears that come fast down my cheeks. Zoë, she's here somehow and she's propping me up, my pulse in my head thundering a hurricane. Her lips are moving and I'm in some strange dream.

"Lu?" she says, as if through a tunnel. "C'mon, Butler, snap back to me."

And I crane my head over to catch the crazy fear in her eyes. Somehow, for some reason, I smile. And then my stomach is lurching, skipping, jumping ship. Mutiny.

And my battered body is heaving forward, thick waves of golden Corona mixed with Reese's and Marta's hippie nut patties hurl from my wide-open throat, out, across the driveway in a magnificent arc. As if in slow motion, I watch as it fans and then finally splatters all over shiny blue paint, slowly revolving chrome rims.

"Jack!" Zoë howls, covering her mouth, and I'm doubled over, gagging, gasping, waves of nausea rippling tides over my skin. And I'm soaked in sweat again, drenched. My innards clench and I hurl again, hit her whip *again*. This time, it sticks, slides down so, so slow. And I'm pretty sure now this isn't a dream. This is real. I retch, cough, spit.

And Zoë's behind me, gripping my hair. "She shoots, she scores," she says soft and a giggle from somewhere deep within my toes surfaces.

"Rinse and repeat," I manage to choke, hacking out gooey strands of saliva, wiping at my face with the front of my shirt. My shoulders shake with a deep-down laugh and Zoë rubs a warm hand over my back.

"Truer words."

"What the flip just happened?" I say, my words massive slow.

"You passed out?" she says, and I slump down onto my knees. "And then you woke up, grinned, and yakked all over my whip." I look at her. "It was massive intense. *Massive*."

"You mean, I didn't die? I'm not actually *dead*?"

She shakes her head. "Sorry, Jack. Not this time." I clutch my ribs. They feel bruised, beaten, bloodied. "And I'm not sure, but you maybe just saved your Oma's goddamn life."

"I didn't save her life. Just shot her some happy juice."

"Whatevs. It was total gladiator. Like, whoa." She steadies me by my arms and we stand together. "Think you're maybe done, there, champ? Giving the whip an ole-fashioned power wash?" and I manage to smile. She leads me to the stairs and we sit. My head drops in my hands.

"Lu," she says. "I gotta ask. Did you take something, pills, anything? Are you back on the kick?"

I shake my head. "No, Jack. I promise. Sauce, yes. But nothing hard. I swear. I think I had a panic attack. Or something. Marta was getting them as a wee-Jack. Right after Mom left. Terrifying."

She sighs. "You certainly had something."

"And now everything smells like vomit."

"Sure does."

I look at her and there she is, right by my side. "I can't

believe you're here." She smiles. "Seriously, thanks for show-ing up, Zo. You really came through." My eyes fill again, bottomless wells of self-sorrow.

"Course," she says, slipping an arm around my shoulder. "That's what apple-Jacks are all about."

I breathe in, feel the spin of the world, the tilt of the axis, the distant pull of the sun. I close shut my eyes.

"Zoë," I say, realizing what I'm about to say before I have time to stop.

"Jack?"

It's now or never, do or die.

"Zo, I think there's another reason I had the attack. Like, not just 'cause of Oma. And it's why I've been MIA and a lame-as-ducks apple-Jack."

"'Kay."

I take another breath, push my fingertips into the pound-ing rhythm of my temples.

"I'm in love."

She laughs. "That'll do it."

"With Eve Brooks. Zo, I think I love her."

Silence. And more silence. I spit a few remnant chunks of dinner into the shrubbery.

"And she broke my goddamn heart."

The line goes total dead. Crickets and tumbleweed, the whole nine.

After lifetimes, centuries, Zoë speaks.

"One thing about you, Butler . . ." I swivel, look at her. "You never cease to surprise."

"Word?" I choke out.

"Word."

Zoë calls Maya. She rallies the troops. They're an army for my one and my flag beats the wind at half-mast as Taps and a twenty-one gun salute pounds in my ears and I'm a prisoner of my own war. I spill the whole damn story, from Raine Hall to Ms. Hayes, the whole, pathetic reel of my secret, sad-sack, so-called love life. I say I haven't told this stuff to anyone. That maybe I got used to it, to being secret and alone. And then I plow onward, to my present descent into wretchedness and Eve's illicit dinner with Nate Gray, ending it all on where we began, the infamous e.p.t. in the betties' bathroom. I tell them they can never tell a soul about the e.p.t. and Zoë says, straight-faced, "Her secret is safe, Jack, as we are your bosom friends. The friends of your bosom."

And Maya doesn't even blink. Until she does and she's crying all over the goddamn car, saying how massive sorry she is for me, about everything, about how hard it's been and how she loves the gays and thinks each and every one is a special angel. Which is . . . interesting. She takes it all on, feeling for herself every blip and blunder along my windy, wayward way. And I don't even tell her to can it. 'Cause that's Maya, bleeding heart and all.

Then Zoë gets hooked on Eve cracking on me and calling up Nate Gray. For that, she says, Eve Brooks must die. I don't even tell her how much I disagree. 'Cause that's Zoë—a tough nut, hard as rocks. My rock.

Then I'm thinking of Eve and Oma, and my hands start shaking again. Maya gives me a hug, says she wishes I'd told them sooner. Zoë gets quiet and says she wonders if maybe I didn't tell her 'cause she's always acting a flap-Jack, saying *that's gay* and all, and she looks about ready to cry. I smile, squeeze her arm, and say, "I forgive you, Jack, as you are my bosom friend. The friend of my bosom."

And I know the Cats are gonna be okay.

Get on Up, Jack

First, we're Bowling Alley Cats.

Eve and Maya say, "Word, Lu. You're up!"

I say, "Easier said than done."

They say, "You know we massive love you."

I say, "Sorry, Jacks. That's a rough lot."

They smile and hug me. They say, "Apple-Jack, it'll be beat."

I say, "I'm losing my marbles."

They say, "What d'you need?"

I say, "I'd like to volunteer my skull as a bowling ball, please."

Maya pulls us, heels dragging in the dirt, to yoga. I salute the sun. I'm warrior one, two, and three. I'm tree, lion, and lotus. I get massive into noose. Small drip drops drip from my eyes and pool and spatter on my sticky, spongy blue mat. I ain't nothing but a downward-facing dog, c-cryin' all the time.

Zoë says, "Get on up, Jack, and let's slice."

She drags me away from Oma's house and tosses threads on my bed and helps me get my superfreeze fly on and takes us to a massive hit club in the city, sliding a fake into my rear skinnies' pocket. My apple-Jacks push their pinkies to the roof and clink thin-stemmed martinis as I chug deep-seated shots of tequila. We slice and they mingle and flirt, the rhythmic hammering engulfing the sorry blips knocking faintly in my heavy, sodden heart cage.

We bounce into Clarissa, Molly Master Jack, and she pulls me into the bathroom, her eyes cat-glossy and dilated. "Butler," she says, "rock 'n' roll," and fishes three pills with stars, smileys, and hearts from her back pocket. But Zoë crashpads in, giving Clarissa the stink eye, pulling me away even though my heart aches for the happy daffy high sleeping soft in that sweet hit candy.

I crash out, slump heavy on a cold curb by the entrance and Zoë comes out, says Maya's found her future husband. I shake my head and she sits by my side and wipes away black blurs from my raccoon eyes.

"Flash Flood Area," I say.

"Slippery When Wet." She slings her arm around my shoulders.

The rhythm of the night thunders on without us, and then Maya's sinking down beside us, looking dejected.

"Wedding's off?" I say and she gives me a soft flick on my arm.

"Shavers are skuzz. Caution: Dead End." She catches my eye. "And betties, too. I'm an equal opportunity hater."

I try a smile.

"Never was final sale on those Pretty Pennies," Zoë says, dragging deep a tar.

"Not to be trusted." Maya nods.

Zoë looks at me, pulls on a grin. "Hey, Jack. Remember that time when you schemed Mrs. Gallagher's magenta high heels from her closet and sported them all through calc and she never knew?"

I laugh, sniffle. Laugh again.

"Or what about that time when I knocked Holly Malone in the mug in gym class 'cause she slide-tackled you from behind?"

I sniffle, laugh a little more.

Maya says, "Or when I was coma on mono and you Jacks licked my spork and we spent January of freshman year on three-way dialing, scarfing tea and popcorn over clash-trash daytime soaps?"

I smile. "And that time we all got massive blazed at Blue Lake and got hit with those Betty Scouts, spazzing around all day with them, snagging flutterbies in nets?"

We laugh and laugh and laugh.

And I cry and cry and cry.

Maya and I are heeling it by the river. Zoë's off the clock, getting into some dram-o-rama with Gideon at his house. We walk, quiet, and follow a dusty trail along the slick-black, rolling river.

"I'm so flip, My," I say. "Lost. A heap," and she smiles with a sad tug at her mouth, rubs a mitt over my back. "Why would Eve pull this? Why is she into that cog again?"

Maya's hush. She walks dragging a crooked stick in a line through the dirt. She looks at me. "Maybe she's not. Maybe she's just scared."

"I dunno. She said she wasn't. She said those words." I shake my head. "Why should she be?"

"'Cause." She smiles. "That's how I'd feel."

"But I'm not gonna hurt her."

"No. That's not it. She's scared of herself. Of who she is if she's heart-Jacks with you. And scared of hurting you."

"Word," I sigh. "She's doing a massive beat job of it for not wanting to."

Maya's hush.

I look at her. "What?"

"No, nothing. I s'pose I think you should dial her. I know Zoë's out for blood. But I think Eve deserves a chance to scat. Give her a shot to explain."

I'm sullen and flip. My heart cage rises and falls, burning and raw. "But she lied, My."

"Word."

I sigh massive deep. "Okay. But what if she won't scat with me?"

"She will."

"How d'you know?"

"Because," she says. "I would."

Illuminated

"I was so flip," Eve says. "I dialed her when the sun came up and she told me to heel it on over.

We're sitting on the hood of my heap-a-junk banger hatchback, shoulder to shoulder, Eve munching her morning bagel. Her mom opens the front door and waves as she strolls to her mailbox and snags the morning paper. We're hush and smile and wait for her to leave. Beneath my sailor hat, my skull whirls with words. My anger stirs and yanks at my chest.

"Why did you lie?" I say, on edge. Her arm stiffens and pulls away. "I would've been hit."

"No. I don't think you would've."

I shrug, trying to lift the hurt hanging like chains around my neck. "This is massive hard," I say. "This whole just-scatting-with-Nate-to-figure-stuff-out thing is rough for me."

"Word," she says. "Me too." She scowls and licks her gorgeous lips. "I'm flip in the skull. What can I say?"

"You can say . . ." I tap my cheek with my finger. "You can say you'll only scat with me. Ever." I glance out of the corner of my eye.

"Eggs, Beatstreet. You got it."

"And you can say Nate Gray is a Blimp-Skull-McPopsicle-Mug and you'll never see him again."

"He does have a big skull," she laughs. "Word. He's a Blimp-Skull."

"McPopsicle-Mug . . . ," I prompt.

She smiles mop sad at me.

I finish, ". . . who I'm never gonna see again. Ever. Or scat with. Ever."

She looks at me, resting her chin on her open palm. "I can't say that."

I sigh. The noose of my anger dissolves and I'm hacked

and feel wiped clean. Like something's changing. "I'm sorry I didn't trust you."

"I'm sorry I lied." I watch her as she takes a big bite from her bagel. A car drives by, honks its horn. Eve looks up.

"You seem different," I say. "Or something." She looks at me, tilts her head.

"How so?"

"Well, you're, like, eating. That's one thing."

"I suppose I am."

"Yeah?"

"Crisscross my heart."

"How come?"

"I'm hungry?" she laughs and I shove my shoulder into hers. "I'm happy, too—or at least, getting there. I'm happy you called me," and she smiles soft golden suns. "When I'm happy, I eat."

"Being with Nate didn't make you happy?"

She sighs, looks down at her lap. "Sometimes it did, in the get-go. But looking back on it now, it was like he was erasing me to see himself more clearly. And I was letting him. If that makes any sense."

"Um."

"I mean, it was like I didn't wanna take up space. If I did, then he'd see all the flip things about me I knew he thought were ugly, boring, whatever. After a while, I told him this was okay. So I just didn't eat and got smaller and smaller and harder to see. So he could become bigger, easier to see."

I can't imagine this. I had no idea.

She goes on. "But last night, with Nate. It was kind of amazing."

My veins and arteries go cold. "Oh?" I manage.

She nods. "I think it's why I flipped on you, told you not to come."

I can barely look at her.

"'Cause Nate, he, like, didn't get to me. Or I didn't let him. And it felt so good, but also kind of bad. Like I knew exactly what he wanted from me and I couldn't believe I had ever given it. And he got all pissy, like his trained monkey wouldn't perform. And I could see it. And yeah, I wanted one of us to disappear. But it wasn't me."

I let out the gallons of breath I realize I'm holding in, find her eyes. "Well, it's a good thing I didn't massive tweak and assume the worst."

Eve laughs. "Word. Good thing."

We go quiet, the whole of it, of us, hanging silently between us.

"But, listen, Thumbs," I finally say, clearing my throat, desperately willing away the heartache of it all. "I wrote you this crank, lame-o poem. Like, a million and five days ago. I dunno why I just thought of it. But I have it here."

She holds out her hand and against my better judgment, I slip it from the pouch of my hoodie and into her hand. She reads it and I look away, smooth down my bangs, my face burning red-hot. Spell a few sentences of the poem in my head. None of them fit. When I turn back, she's looking at my lips.

"I wanted to kiss you just then," she says.

"If a kiss is an idea, it should just be a kiss."

Her mouth opens in a laugh and she grabs me, heeling it to the side of the house where she pulls me by my earlobes and presses me into the plastic siding and her smiling eyes cross just a little bit and she kisses me. In the broad orange light at the cusp of daybreak, her mouth, her smell, her touch, warm my chill and cloak my sorrow. I'm horizon and she's sun and we are joined as the day is just begun.

We are illuminated.

⸻

We sit cross-legged on her futon to share the dregs of a stick of canna pinched tight between tweezers. I fool about rolling the canna with my flip poem and Eve says, "You touch that thing and I'll ax you, Bug-Jack."

She flicks my Zippo on and off on her leg—a trick I taught her.

I sink into the smoke and rub at the rough sting of my rattling heart cage.

"I sorta feel like someone took a garden hoe and scraped the insides of my chest out," and Eve looks at me with big, sad eyes, the canna in her digits glowing red and hot. I tell her about my panic attack and yakking all over Zoë's car. I tell her about telling my Jacks about her and how I had to shoot Oma with the morphine and nearly lost my marbles in the meantime. I try and laugh it off, say, "It's been a real peach of a week."

Then we go silent and I start picking at a scab till it bleeds. She slaps my fingers away and I grab her wrist, count the freckles marching up and down the crests of her knuckles. I say I wonder what *freckle* tastes like and try and gnaw the ridge of her thumb. She smiles, says maybe we still need to talk about stuff.

I shake my head.

"Okay," she says. "Well, whaddya wanna talk about, then?"

I shrug. "Good recipes for freckle? I mean, what kind of wines pair best? Red or white? I don't know."

"Nate?" she says.

"Nope."

"College?"

"No."

"Gun control?"

"Um."

"Okay." She smiles. "Masturbation," and I choke, cough, wheeze, nearly die. Then Eve's cracking up and she lays the canna down smoking in a vast white oyster shell spotted with our ash. Her cheeks flush red. "I do it," she says, daring me with a look and I'm silent. I'm a pin, not dropping. Her smile goes broad. "Like, *a lot.*"

My heart skips hopscotch in its cage.

This is revolution.

"Like, *a lot?*" I say, looking down at my guilty mitts lying in my lap.

"Maybe," she laughs.

Blood rushes to my face. "You know," I say softly, "I think we have that in common."

She's silent. She takes my hand and pushes it down the front of her skinnies and my hand and I slide into the warmest pair of jeans in America.

"Well then," she says into my ear, her breath coming quick. "You'll be a pro."

My fingers fall into her.

She's so wet, she's electric. She's anemone and I am clown and I swim gently into her stunning embrace.

Misty Ginger Haze

Eve sips her mug of hot honey-ginger and her cheeks flush McIntosh Red, a sweet, early fruit. We're on hour number fifteen plus fifty-five-minutes straight together. But really, who's counting? I bend to kiss the flat caps of her knees and she grins, laughing through a ginger fog at my googly-for-you eyes.

My Misty Ginger Haze.

She shakes her head, smiling, and sips her tea. I inhale her skin. I tell her she's ripe for picking and she falls from the tree. I wander like a grazing Holstein through fall-blazoned orchards and take her in my mouth and swallow her whole. I'm drunk. I wobble and hiccup. I am holy cow.

Eve says, "It's crazy. I dunno why it never occurred to me to get into it with a betty. But I'm switch as a clam it has."

"You're switch as a clam I occurred to you, little mollusk Thumbs?"

"So switch," she says, yanking me down into her warm nets.

I'm a fool moon in her galaxy arms. She teaches me gravity.

I am lap cat. Hear me purr.

Like Home

I'm rocking real slow in a chair by Oma's bed. She hasn't woken at all today, hasn't eaten a thing. I prod at my throat and the hard swelling of my glands. I think I'm getting sick. No shocker after the marathon couple of weeks I've had.

I watch Oma's chest, rising and falling, the peaceful blips of her meter chiming away. My eyes slowly shut, when my speak vibrates in my pocket and I see Eve's called, no message left. Strange, I think. Massive.

I'm about to dial her back, a funny feeling in my gut, when I hear a rustling at the door and look to see Dad standing there, smiling. He strolls over, leaning by Oma's bed to give her a small kiss on her forehead and to pick up a bottle and capped syringe. "Upping her dose again tonight," he sighs. "Won't be long now."

I stand and again glance at my speak. I feel Dad watching me and I look up, tuck it into my jeans.

"Eve?" he asks and I nod, feeling the stiffness in my neck, vaguely wondering how he knew it was her. I swallow, my throat raw. I'm getting sick, for sure. Dad smiles, stepping close to pull me into a bear hug. I hug him back and it feels good, like home.

"Dad," I say into the fabric of his shirt. "I think I'm—"

He nods his head and hugs me tighter. "I know, sweetie. I know."

I pull away, look up at him. "Huh?"

"What?"

"No," I laugh. "What were you gonna say?"

He furrows his brow. "What were *you* gonna say?"

"*Dad.*"

He smiles, looking infinitely tired.

"That you're gay, Luce. That's what I was gonna say," and I feel my mouth drop open as a dry, hot laugh escapes from the vast desert of my soul.

"That's not what . . ." I reach up to prod my swollen glands. "Never mind."

He pushes my fingers away and presses his own into the rocklike lumps of my throat. He pokes around and finally nods his head.

"Yep. You also have glands." I can barely look him in the eye. "And it's possible you're getting sick."

I nod, then Dad and I, we go quiet and stare down at Oma, my brain working to reconcile the swirling bits of shrapnel ricocheting around. But suddenly it just doesn't seem to matter. And my thoughts, they dim to a quiet rustle and outside, the dogwood branches beat a steady rap against the window. I feel Dad peeking at me from the corner of his eye, his hands jingling the change in his pocket.

Such a Dad thing to do.

"Also," I say, my voice quiet, "I don't think I wanna study medicine. I sort of hate it, actually. I wanna do something else. Write, maybe. I dunno."

He smiles. "We'll talk about it."

I look at him and he seems so cool, so calm. It occurs to me then, in that quiet moment, how much I love him. How much he is going through losing his mom. And, how hard it'll be when it's his pulse on the line and I'm swimming around in his big shoes, saying goodbye to the one person who knows and loves you most in the whole entire world. In the living room, someone coughs and the TV is flicked on.

"So, it's not a big deal to you, then? Like, all of it?" And

Dad just shrugs, shakes his head. "Well," I say, taking a breath. "That was certainly an anticlimax," and he's chuckling, giving my arm a quick squeeze.

"Love you."

"Love you, too."

Marco Polo

Eve's on the speak, clip-clop crying. When she answered, I thought someone had hoisted her phone because I almost didn't recognize her voice.

She snuffles and heaves, telling how she was at a toaster, but now she's heeling it home on foot through musty wooded streets. The rest of the world dreams and drools while she walks, clip-clop-clip, drip-drop-drip.

They invited her out. The other three Pretty Pennies.

They said, "EB! Betty-Jack, we miss you! We haven't seen you in years! We massive feel like you hate us!" They also said, "Don't bring anyone." She didn't know that meant don't bring me. She didn't know why she said she'd go. She didn't know why she went.

She arrived and there they were, dressed to the nines, tens, and back again, coy and smiling slimy snail-slow grins. They gave her bony shoulder half hugs and quick escorted her, stealth-mode, from the backyard teeming with hormonally drenched toaster-goers to the fluorescent-lit kitchen. They all sat down.

They said, "We know."

She said, "You know what?"

They stared and stared. A crank clock on the wall cooed Morning Dove O'clock.

"We're not the only Jacks who know," said the Blond One.

"But you're safe. The Jacks who saw promised they haven't spilled to a soul," said the Black-Shagged One.

"They came straight to us, as your apples. They knew we'd wanna be the first to know," said the Two-Timing Brunette.

But Eve was crickets. She sat still as a rail, petrified wood.

"You should just come out and spill it," they said. "Admit what you are."

She shrugged. "I really dunno what you want me to spill."

"Just admit you're, like, a *lesbian* now," and their pointy-perfect noses scrunched at the word's unpleasant aroma.

"Some Jacks scoped you two." The Blond One was a blur of straw and rouge.

"And we scoped you together last week at the lake." The Black-Shagged One's mug was sketched in blotchy black ink.

"Those Jacks couldn't believe it. They spilled you were *kissing*." The Brunette was so sharp and bright, she stung.

Eve just sat there, silent, smarting, imagining our once beatstreet kisses, now infinite galaxies away, shooting through milky ways, dripping white with menace and shame.

———

Eve's on the speak, clip-clop crying and I cut a wheel fast, but our connection is shoddy. I'm Marco. She's Polo.

Marco? Polo!

Marco? Polo!

Marco?

Her voice crackles on the line and then is gone.

"I'm heelin' it to get you. Where are you?" I ask into dead air.

Call lost.

I wind and twist and speed around familiar suburban streets, the road's curves burnt into my skull, a map of my wee-Jack life. I squint into the vivid glare of high-beamed asphalt and imagine I see the silhouette of her back in every mailbox, shrub, and sign I pass. Reception's three bars too few, my deduction and intuition the only GPS I've got. But I'm determined to scope her walking through this dark and hollow night.

As I wheel, I imagine dramatic confrontation. I imagine retribution. Gale-force winds, I envision I whip through their toaster of entangled twosomes and flip-cupping contestants, to the three Pretty Penny Queenettes.

"Revolution!" I scream.

I holler a great howling bawl, a thick and muscled bluetick coonhound, my three masked and ring-tailed raccoon targets scatter and chatter and cower in a looming shadowy corner. In a last-ditch dash for life, the Yellow-Eyed Jack leaps screaming on my skull. The Black-Eyed Jack scurries and spits and hooks her razor-edged teeth in my ankle. The Brown-Eyed Jack surges, viscous threads salivating for my jugular. But each clash-Jack's met with my Jaws of Life and Death and I lift them high in my crushing crane grip and drop them, tails swishing, claws closing around wind into a deep crank pit of trash-compacting crushers.

I'm jolted to reality when I scope a frail silhouette. It's Eve. I roll up slowly beside her, and she raises her skull in bright lights, teary, black streaks slicing down white cheeks, her eyes caught fierce in fright. She softens when she scopes my mug and she chokes, sobbing. I pull off the road and she's opening the door and sliding into my banger.

Back at my house, Eve crawls heavily into my bed. She curls in, feet tangling between sheets and quilt and I sit by her head, wind my digits into her fever-damp hair.

I kick off my boots and lie beside her. Thick sobs rack through her small, sad frame, and I wrap my worn nets about her ribs. She turns, curling hot and wet into my achy breaky heart cage and I hold her, rub slowly her fire-hot back. Her fists curl in tight clash knots, her thumbs tucked under coiled fingers. Fisherman's knots. I think I know how to untie them, but I can't. She shivers and sweats, sweet and yeasty, like baking bread. A swampy thing, she's moss and secret places.

A fine dew of moisture fills the space between her face and mine and I kiss her eyelids and wipe her nose. She turns her face from mine. We lie, fitting like cups and saucers, me her spoonful of medicine. I tuck my face in the crook of her neck and breathe her sweet, sad sorrow.

I rock her soft. I rock her as she drifts and I rock her as she sleeps and I rock her as she wakes, burning like live coals next to me. She lies, lost and adrift, an infinity stretching between us.

free fall

Eve and I are ghostly hush, chowing granola the next morning when Dad schleps into the crickets kitchen, says he needed his computer, hasn't done any paperwork in a week. He gets into poking around our abandoned abode, dumping out expired milk, tossing moldy bread. He finally gets hit to our vibe, giving me a concerned, fatherly glance, but I look away. He says it's time for him to jet.

Eve shudders slowly to life, her arms wrapping a fortress around her shaky frame. "I'm so sorry to hear 'bout your mum," she says as Dad is pulling his laptop onto his shoulder, scooping up his keys. He smiles a thin line, deep shadows under his eyes.

"Thanks, Evie," he says. He looks at me again, then leaves.

***

Eve and I, we cut a wheel across town, still hush, and I pull up in front of her house. She pushes open the door, but doesn't get out. She sighs, sits back against her seat.

"After all this," she says, "I think I'm gonna need some time."

I wanna throw up. I nod and stare at the taut wrap of leather enveloping the steering wheel.

"Hey," she says. I lift my heavy head and see her eyes are leaden and pink and her face is flushed and soft around the edges. I smile weak and my eyes are hot and brimming. But I don't protest. I don't scream and yell. I don't get jammed or kiss her or tell her I love her. I just blink away my tears and look up at the ceiling.

"I get it. I really do."

"Word, Bug," she says and slides out of my banger.

She's miles away.

***

Dad's home when I get there and he's sitting on the screen porch, coat still on, laptop in its case on the floor.

"You still here?" I say and he nods, pats the couch beside him.

"Marta and Miles are with the others, they're grabbing brunch in the city."

We sit in silence, green-bellied hummingbirds dive-bombing like fighter jets from feeder to flower and back again. Their wings buzz, a tight, hard noise. I close my eyes and flop back my head. Dad lifts an arm over my shoulders and I lean into the solid weight of him. "So," he says. "Wanna tell me what happened?"

And from deep within me, sobs like a freight train rack clickety-clack through my torso, tears pushing warm springs onto my hotplate cheeks. He pulls me close and kisses the top of my head and I tell him my tale as he holds me light, like the catching of a feather from infinite free fall.

He pulls his fingers through my hair just like Mom used to when I was a wee-Jack and my eyes slide shut and I wonder if she touched him like this, if that's why he knows how.

As I'm nodding off, Dad pulls a blanket from the back of the couch over me, sighing heavy. And before I know it, I'm startling awake to the ring of his speak. I peel open my lids and he's yawning, rubbing world-weary eyes. And then he's talking and his voice goes soft, strained, and I know right away it's Oma.

We pull into her drive and there are no other cars. They're on their way, Dad says. He cuts the engine and looks at me.

"Maybe this doesn't make sense right now, but it sounds to me like Eve needs a friend."

I shake my skull, clip off my seat belt. "She said she needed time."

He pushes open his door. "Well, it's my opinion we don't always know what we need. If you really like this girl, you're gonna have to fight." And he's climbing out, leaning in through the open window

"But that's all I've been doing, Dad. I'm hacked. Spent."

He lifts his large, flat palms. "Welcome to love, *Jack*." And he heels it inside. I sit for a spell, then flip open my speak to type.

miss u

Dad and I sit vigil, the nurse perched in her chair by the corner, Dad and I each holding one of Oma's hands. With my other, I run a finger along Bitsy's stout little fox-like snout. The Beeps are slow, lifetimes elapsing between each. Her breathing, loud under her oxygen mask, sounds gravelly, pinched, labored.

And I always imagined that when this happened, I would be floating, watching from somewhere far, far above. But I'm right here, everything in full focus.

I feel it all. And Oma's so real, so right now, so painfully real.

Fifteen minutes in, my speak goes off. I slip it out to put it on silent and see it's Eve. I stare at the screen, watch as I miss her call. She buzzes back.

miss u 2

I slide it back in my pocket and Dad catches my eye. He gives a sad smile, tears rolling gently down his cheeks.

"Eve?" he says.

I look at the floor.

"Go," he says.

"No way. I can't leave you now."

But he just shakes his head. "I'm fine," he says so soft. "Oma loved you kids so much. She always said . . ." And we're suspended in a moment, Dad and I. He tilts his head, gestures for the door. "I'd like to say goodbye before everyone arrives. Just me and Mum."

"Dad, c'mon. This is crazy." But he shakes his head.

"Go. I'm asking you to leave."

I watch him, wait for him to change his mind. But I see he won't. I lean down to Oma and kiss the fuzzy white crown of her head. Take one last look at her face, her hands, the crest of her knees under the blanket, her tiny feet in oversized socks. The gentle, slow rise and fall of her chest.

I stand, give Dad a hug.

And I walk away.

Mission Possible

I motor to Eve's. Minutes, eons, light-years go by and I pull into her drive, knowing I better make this count. Knowing this is it, everything or nothing on the line. I don't know how I know, but I do. I dial her number, and when she answers, she's groggy and her breath is heavy in the earpiece. Upstairs, in her attic room, I see the gentle breeze of her curtain flapping in her open window.

I wait. Eve opens the door and steps outside, wrapping her arms and sweater tight around her body as she heels it up to my banger. My headlights illuminate her small frame. I roll down my window. I ask her to cut a wheel with me.

"Where to?" She shivers in thin pajamas.

"Cape Cod," I say. "Truro."

She pauses. "That's, like, four hours away."

I nod. I'm Double O Seven, Eight, and Nine and she's my Mission Possible.

Eve licks her lips. "If I come with, this doesn't change anything, Bug. You know that, right? Really," she says.

"I'm hit, Thumbs. Whatever you need."

"Word," she finally says. "Let's jet."

Like a Rolling Stone

How does it feel?

*H*ow *does it feel?*
    We cut a wheel into the day's blinding noon, to old, folksy tunes with raspy vocals and harmonica, strumming guitar ringing clear. The rough, leathery layers of hurt and sorrow peel slow in thin slices off our weary-teary eyes as the sun makes its highest ascent and winks and flashes sharp off the passing bogs and marshes.

To be without a home.

We drive and drive and land in an alternate universe. Sunny, bright vacation station, T-shirt stands, SUVs, over-priced seafood shacks, billowing twenty-foot rainbow-colored flags. We score a campsite at a park I remember from larger, long-ago past days and we buy a bundle of wood for a beach fire and some bread and cheese and fruit from a rustic little shop. We unpack. Pole A slides into D and F into B and our tent's up 'n ' at 'em and our sleeping bags are thrown in and unrolled like caterpillars.

Like a complete unknown.

We heel the short walk through piney wooded trails I remember like dreams, our flip-flops flip-flopping. The sweet musk of bayberry perfumes our path and highbush blueber-ries speckle the shrubs and we pick and eat. Eve startles, laughing, when an angry swallow swoops low at our heads as we pass her nest and I wrap my nets around her waist and lift her, curly hair jumping, into the salty summer air.

Like a rolling stone.

The ocean licks the shore and gulls circle and cry. Family-Jacks pack in under striped and spotted umbrellas, lounging behind glaring shades and wide-brimmed hats.

We're quick to the water's edge with toes dipped in the cold, clear sea and soon we're walking our warm bellies under and swimming, gasping through the stiff current of small curling waves. Our ice-cube feet grip the sandy floor as it washes away with each coming swell and Eve curls her legs around mine and we shiver and scope a horizon-bound fishing boat. We hold fast, cheek to freezing cheek.

And you ask, *How does it feel?*

⁓⁓⁓⁓⁓

We sit on our towels by the feet of the rambling dunes. The sand's massive hot on our thighs as the sun beats ultraviolet relief from the sea's deep chill still clinging to our skin and soon we start to scat real life. She tells me about the way the Pennies and Nate make her squirm in her skin. About not eating, how thin she got, her weight in actual, legit digits. It spooks me cold.

We scat and I feel more grown-up than I know I am.

I tell her how I sometimes—but mostly used to—cut, and show her the lines on my arm as proof. I tell her about counting steps and letters and feeling so Ophelia with anxiety I think sometimes my brain might crack. I tell her I got so hooked on alters last year I almost missed the train out of happytown and Eve says it's all okay, I'm all okay. Eve and I, we scat and scat and then fall asleep on our towels with soft, sad smiles on our word-weary lips.

⁓⁓⁓⁓⁓

We heel it back to our campsite slow, counting together the now 162 steps where it used to be 240 of my own, small wee-Jack strides.

"This was Oma's favorite place on the planet," I say. "This land, washed-away dunes, lighthouses moaning, houses swept away in storms."

And our nets swing with our steps, our digits spun fast together, knuckles and palms gritty with salty dust.

And I smile. "Remember that time when I came up to you on the beach and brought you a stinking white ray and you fed me cantaloupe and I asked you if you remembered all those times?" I say and Eve, she laughs liquid silver.

"I do," she says. "I so do."

How Can I Say?

How can I say what it is to feel the weight of the betty you love as she naps, her arms and legs draped and entwined with your own, her breath coming in short bursts of warm air against your neck?

How can I say what it is to think and see in poetry, to scope the sky and ground in short phrases that drip and heave with blood and bones and dust?

How can I say what it is to know the heat of your heart-Jack pressed hard into the corners of your own, moving and rocking, musk mingling with pine and wood smoke, the dew on her back shimmering and rising, meeting in a cloud the breath of a cool night's air?

How can I say what one does with eyes so gray and clear you heel it on foggy sands and are lost and found and lost again, your reflection ebbing, mirrored in the glassy pool of her luminous hazy gaze?

How can I say what it is to hold someone so close they move through you and beyond and emerge sliding fast into an eclipsing vastness your steps can never retrace?

Starry Sheets

We've got one last night together. We've decided to spend it (illegally) on the beach.

We heel it with our sleeping bags, a picnic dinner, pillows, the Sunday paper, and three small logs over the still-warm dunes and onto the beach. The full moon is hung and its glow illuminates our pilgrimage from tent to shore.

We heel it by the water's black slapping edge, the sand glinting silver specs, the palms of our feet knowing tumbled rocks and shells. We veer back into the dunes and scope a sheltered inlet where the breeze is hush and warm.

We dig together a small pit and our digits find damp, cool sand and crank little clear-skinned shrimps jump and scatter. We arrange crumpled newspaper, small drifted sticks, and our three logs like a tepee and spark it with a match. I blow massive careful on each pocket of flame as Eve pokes and prods. Our fire ripens and we smile happyfaces, and lean back on our heels, brushing sand from our mitts and knees.

We lay a sleeping bag down, unzip and spread it out. Pillows next. Then us. We pull a second, plaid-lined bag over our chilly skin and are a sandy sandwich and we squirm and smile and link legs and nets and lips. The fire spits and crackles and we roll and twist under our starry sheets.

We're skin to skin and my hands trace her warm curves and chasms. She's a smiling shadow as she squirms, pushing apart my legs, and disappears. She isn't sight or sound or smell. She's touch. Her fingers are on me first, light and slippery. Then her mouth, soft and sure, and my eyes slip closed and I find spaces in myself I didn't know. Her fingers slide in and whole continents, green and rocky, desert and jungle, rise up from my core. Hot blushes pulse through me and my oceans open their shores. And soon I'm close, her hands joining my rolling rhythms, and I swim submerged, deep in my new planet's waters. I can see land. And I submit and a final, powerful tide rushes in.

I have arrived.

I gasp and open my eyes and she rises to greet me, her nets wrapping sweaty and fast around my steaming frame. I laugh and she kisses my rosy face and my swollen mouth and she rocks me in time to the Atlantic's steady roll.

Piss and Vinegar

With the sun's morning mug comes reality. We're two flip birds to daybreak's one stone and dread circles high like gulls over a sinking ship.

We traipse back to our campsite mitt in mitt, salty beach dew clinging to our skin in crumbling white dust, our bedding slung in soggy heaps over our shoulders. We dismantle our campsite and pack our junk into my banger.

Rain falls in fat drops as we cut a wheel across the towering, fog-bound bridge and find chow in a crank little seaside café. I'm massive in-n-out, moping through break-fast and Eve says, "Let's see that happyface," and I scrunch my nose and show my teeth and we laugh and smile sad over a shared plate of grease, hash browns, and fried eggs. We take hot tea to go.

Back in my banger, we pass the steaming cup back and forth and slowly unwrap the hard facts of our sad state. Evil hit-Jacks, crossing enemy lines, small-town cogs jiving massive smack, ex-heart-Jacks. The vast unknow-able future. College. We both leave in three weeks.

I laugh and say, "If we ever start a band, we can call our-selves A Rock and a Hard Place."

"Or, The Devil and the Deep Blue Sea?"

"Word," I say. "Or how 'bout Piss and Vinegar—but I call being Vinegar." She laughs and her voice is cool aloe on my scorched heart.

But we're no badrats. We're true-blue betties wheeling it home in a banger speeding in two directions at once, and as I catch her smiling eyes over the steaming tea, I know she'll always be my Misty Ginger Haze.

We pull back onto the main road and my speak buzzes in. It's Dad.

"Oh," I say when Marta's voice is on the other line. "Word."

She laughs. "Word to you, too, flap-Jack."

"Oma?"

"Yeah," she says.

"Yeah. Miles all right?"

"He's my human tissue." I smile, glad she's home. "So," she says after a beat. "Rumor is you're like some big lez-Jack now."

"Um."

"With Eve Brooks, nonetheless," Marta says. "Such an ace." And then we're both cracking up. "That's beat, Jack," she says. "I gotta heel. Dad just wanted me to let you know. And check you're still alive."

"Still kicking." I pause. "Thanks, Sister."

"Word."

We hang up and I look at Eve and I see in her eyes she understands Oma's gone. She runs a palm up and down my arm and I surrender the helm. I'm speak, not think.

"Hey, Thumbs. Whaddya say?"

"Whaddya say what?"

"Let's just jump in. See if we can't make this thing work." She looks back out her window and I plow on. "Long-distance phone calls, plane tickets, massive expensive speak bills. We gotta at least try." But Eve's gone hush. She sighs deep, hot steam billowing from her cup. "A Jack's gotta think about her future every once in a while, y'know."

Her lips curl into a small smile but her eyes are still down. I watch the road, my heart cage pounding away with the swish-swosh-swish of the windshield wipers. I tell myself I tried.

I'm getting good and sweaty-palmed and my crank

heart's a sinking ship as the dashed white lines whip under the hood of my wheeling banger. But then Eve's nodding her head. Slow and then more quick, and she's a massive smile out of the corner of my eye. I'm pulling off the road and P is for Park and she's crying and pulling my earlobes, her eyes crossing just a tiny bit as she presses her beatstreet nose into mine. She's kissing me, saying, "Yes. Yes, you."

And then we're hush again, nose to nose, and her eyes are big saucers and her mouth is moving miles a minute. She sits back in her seat and rattles off plans all ponies 'n' pigtails about summer fun, Christmas breaks to come, traveling the globe. Us—Bug 'n' Thumbs. I smile, watching her, and start back up my banger and D is for Drive and we accelerate and we're cutting a wheel forward.

"I love you," I say, so softly she can't hear over the crank hum of the engine, and I take her hand and it's soft and warm, like dawn.

I take a massive deep breath.

I am anew.